About The Author:

The author is dead.

Long live the author.

IF YOU CAN DRAW ME

A Novel By Zee

This first edition published in 2024 by Me & Zee Publishing

A Cataloging in Publication record for this book is available from the National Library of Australia.

E-book ISBN: 978-0-6486049-0-7
Paperback ISBN: 978-0-6486049-1-4
Hardback ISBN: 978-0-6486049-2-1

There are two different fonts for two different narrative voices.

For Dolly's voice, I chose the serif font, EB Garamond (2011) by Georg Duffner and Octavio Pardo.

For David's voice, I chose the sans-serif font, Lato (2010) by Warsaw-based designer Łukasz Dziedzic. Lato means "Summer" in Polish.

For the titles and drop-caps, I chose the transitional font Playfair Display (2013) by Claus Evers Sørensen.

Printed on creme paper and bound by

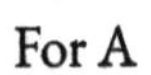

For A

Author's Note

I would like to thank the authors of two German language novels: The Reader and The Piano Teacher. Bernhard Schlink's The Reader was translated into twenty-five languages and was featured in Oprah's Book Club. The novel was adapted into a film in 2008. It received nominations for best film from the British Academy Film Awards, the Golden Globe Awards, and the Academy Awards. Similarly, The Piano Teacher by Elfriede Jelinek received the Nobel Prize for Literature in 2004. The 2001 film adaptation of her novel won the Grand Prix at The Cannes Film Festival. The film was nominated for the best non-English film at the British Academy Film Awards, and best film at the European Film Awards.

These two novels are proof that a story regarding an affair between a teenage boy and a woman twice his age does not disqualify the work from enthusiastic popularity, international publishing, nor prestigious accolades. Accordingly, there should be no reason why my far more modest novel should incur banning, canceling, pearl-clutching, or whatever misguided or feigned outrage that may result from the far less toxic love affair explored herein.

Additionally, thank you to Carson McCullers who wrote The Heart Is a Lonely Hunter. She helped me understand how to articulate the feeling of music into words. I enjoyed her description of Beethoven's Third Symphony.

zee

Author's Note

One

DAVID

The nightmare was always the same. My mother was dead. My father was gone. He took everything with him. The empty space they left behind grew larger the longer I was trapped in the dream. I tore myself free and woke with my heart racing out of my chest. Tears blinding my eyes. I told myself only part of the nightmare was true.

My father left me with his second wife in the city of Chengdu, Szechuan. She and I shared an apartment in a courtyard complex. It was built by the Chinese government where a thousand-year-old temple once stood. Our Soviet-style building was the envy of our neighborhood because it had an elevator. The poured concrete outer wall was plastered with posters of Communist Party Leader Deng Xiaoping and Mickey Mouse. It was 1985.

The old ladies in our complex practiced tai-chi in the courtyard every dawn. Their elegant, deeply lined hands moved slowly in the air as if through water. They mimed the gesture of a white stork spreading her wings, or parting the mane of a wild horse. These gentle graceful moves were deadly attacks in disguise. Some mornings I would make my way down there and join them at the back of the group. The ladies cried out,

'Here comes the *gweilo* (white boy).'

Breakfast was a cup of ginseng tea by the big living room window that refused to open. My father's wife, Mei Mei, arose from her bedroom after me. The sharp scent of her *Double Happiness* brand cigarette was followed by the soft scuffle of her fluffy slippers on the linoleum floor. She entered our living room and wrapped her arms around me from behind. Her body pressed into mine, separated only by the mulberry-silk of her chemise. My father had sent her seven of these nightdresses in seven different colors from his office in Osaka, Japan. Her favorite was the palest shade of pink. It blended with the creamy tint of her skin so she appeared naked. Her long, thick, black waves of disheveled hair brushed against my cheek. I caught her scent, *Opium* by Yves St. Laurent. The perfume was another gift sent from Osaka. She smelled like a gypsy fire of smoldering resin. There were notes of clove, jasmine, frankincense, and a whiff of tobacco. Her smell and touch carried feelings of awkward affection and uneasy arousal. These thoughts wrestled each other in the mud of my fifteen-year-old mind.

I should have gotten to know Mei Mei more than I did. Her name means "little sister". Sadly, I never bothered to ask if she was somebody's little sister. Nor did I show her the most basic courtesy by asking how she met my father. All I had gathered was that she waitressed at three different dumpling restaurants right up until the day they were married. Her voice was high-pitched and child-like. I discovered decades later this was a sign of childhood trauma. If only I had asked more questions. I was afraid of getting too close. I was scared she might be the next parent who abandoned me.

My only insight into her world was her secret stash of English-language erotica she hid deep in her shoe closet. These well-worn books served two purposes. They kept my stepmother company, and they helped me understand sex in a way otherwise impossible in China. Was she as lonely as I was? Occasionally, I would catch her peeling a *Júzi* fruit, separate the segments, and then spend long minutes staring at the detached pieces. Her almond-eyes glazed like a doll's. Her brow furrowed. Her oval face froze, as if she were stuck on a stubborn thought.

She and I were held hostage by my father's absence. He had become less of a loved one and more of an acquaintance. He did not provide for us. It was more accurate to say he sponsored us from three-thousand kilometers away. We were tragic characters from an overwrought Italian opera. We waited for him as Madama Butterfly waited for her thoughtless American husband to sail back to her.

How would we have felt if we already knew he would never return? Japan was about to enjoy an asset price bubble. The whole thing burst in 1992. I found out years later he and his investors made out like bandits. By then, my father started another family elsewhere. We never saw him again.

I filled my days sketching from life around me. The *Itoya* glossless pencils my father ordered from Ginza were never far away from my grip. My art journals were filled with stray cats and dogs, bicycles and brollies, overflowing ashtrays and cups of tea, a folded *People's Daily* and a bootleg cassette. The drawings were a reminder that I was present, that I existed in that time and space. As soon as my school discovered my alleged talent, my curriculum focused on art and very little else. China is like that.

Chengdu was often cloaked in a pall of stifling humidity. When the rain came, the water steamed off the pavement. The yellow sodium-vapor streetlamps fought the gloom. The city was like the set of a French film noir, but *Made in China*. The esplanade along the misty Fuhe River felt no different than a scene from a moody Louis Malle film shot on the Seine. I sketched Chinese women walking along the riverside looking as elegant and brooding as any French femme fatale. My journals were filled with drawings of Chinese ladies as captivating as Jeanne Moreau or Catherine Deneuve.

My greatest challenge was remaining a clandestine observer whilst being the only blonde for miles. As a person-of-no-color, it was difficult to blend in and avoid being noticed whilst noticing everything. To make matters worse, my stepmother kept buying me suspiciously sexy outfits worn by Western teen idols. These ensembles often involved Levi Strauss jeans and leather or denim jackets with sharp showy collars. She ordered them through my father's secretary in Osaka. By the time postage was paid from the States to Japan and finally to China, my clothes tripled in cost. I felt like an expensive *yáng wá wa* (Caucasian doll).

On the day I met Dolly, I was listening to the *Purple Rain* album on my Sony *Walkman*. I was drawing the faces passing by whilst leaning in the doorway of what I thought was a closed shop. The door crashed open. A corpulent white tourist spilled out and barged past me. He reeked of alcohol and disrespect. The man was escorted to the doorway by a striking woman sheathed in a qipao dress the color of Persian turquoise. A curtain of long straight hair fell across one eye. It seemed as if she were hiding something from the world. She held a tall plastic cup of iced tea between the tips of her long fingers. She was a porcelain beauty with a spiderline crack if you looked closely enough, and I was looking. I never stopped looking. I took off my headphones, and was abruptly awake without realizing I was asleep.

The man slurred, 'Thanks a-lot, Lily, the pleasure's all mine.'

'My name is Dolly. Lily is the young one.'

Her words were as smooth as cocoon-spun silk. Her smile was a measured pleasantry.

He phffted.

'All you Orientals look the same to me.'

English was my second language. However, I was sensitive enough to pick up on his ribald tone. I was an old fifteen-year-old.

He swayed in the direction of the Jinjiang Hotel. Dolly held her smile between her lips until he was out of sight, and then dropped it like a guillotine. Her eyes fell to the face I was drawing. She stepped closer to me and stared at my sketch of a woman I saw on the street. Her expression unclenched like an opening fist as she stared into the details of my drawing. Her softening brown eyes moved from the drawing to me. She spoke in perfect Szechuan dialect.

'If you can draw me, I'll give you a free massage.'

The Szechuan language is so soft it melts in your ear. It is said our tongue cools the hottest anger and melts the frostiest heart. I thought the legend was all so much hyperbole until I heard her speak to me like she did.

She gestured for me to follow her through her door. She let me pass close to her body on the threshold, and I caught the scent of her foreign LUX shampoo. She closed the door behind us, and we walked up a cozy stairwell which opened onto an anteroom.

Her place of business was both cheaply and thoughtfully decorated. There were spotted mirrors and plastic flowers in chipped vases, but they were clean and free of dust and harmoniously placed following all the rules of feng shui. She helped me out of my *Wrangler* jacket and hung it by the entry on an iron hook shaped like a woman diving into... somewhere. The art-nouveau ornament matched walls covered in paper printed in a pattern of fleur-de-lys. She guided me to sit in a chair facing away from her. It was a replica of the Arne Jacobsen *Series-7* chair I had only ever seen in a famous photograph. I faced a wall hung with a detailed print of an ancient ink drawing. It was the boudoir scene from a romance called *Dream of the Red Chamber* written during the Qing Dynasty.

I had been growing my hair long like the Western teen idol, Leif Garrett, mostly for Mei Mei's amusement. By the time I matched his long golden locks, Leif had long ago hacked off his mane. Dolly slid a turquoise elastic band from her wrist, yanked back my hair, and tied it into a bun. She was the first person to ever do that to me. With my hair fixed in place, she had full access to my neck. I welcomed the governance she assumed over me.

As soon as she pressed her thumbs into my shoulders, I felt everything let go. She hurt me and healed me with every press into my flesh. I felt beautiful. I felt connected to the world by that strange woman on that strange Saturday afternoon. It was a silly delusion. There was no way the feeling was mutual. She was executing a task as mundane as wiping down a bench, but the effect on me was real.

I was starved for human connection. She would not have known the craving that sat so heavy inside me. I kept it a secret from her, remaining still and silent. When the tips of her long hair brushed my skin, an ocean of endorphins flooded my body. I bit down on the sigh I wanted to let loose. A part of me wished this quiet, intimate transaction would never end. The pleasure was both overwhelming and intimidating. I needed a dialogue, not a monologue. What happened next surprised us both.

I raised my hands to signal for her to stop. She let go of my neck. I rose from the chair and motioned for her to take my place. Her eyes betrayed confusion, but she shrugged her shoulders and took my seat anyway. She settled into the chair, closed her eyes, and let out a long, deep breath.

I took the elastic from my hair and used it to fasten hers into a high, taut ponytail. Fortunately, I had lots of experience fastening hair with Mei Mei. My stepmother's hair was pitch black, a true absence of light. Whereas Dolly's hair shimmered like a raven's wing.

I discovered I was a quick study in the art of massage. Perhaps it is a distant relation to the Tai-Chi I practiced? I found the precise points on her neck, shoulders, and blades that needed kneading. There was a peculiar choreography in the performance of a massage. Hard moves were followed by softness, followed again by hardness. If a massage was music, then an adagio was followed by an allegro.

With the tip of my elbow, I pressed into the space between her nape and left rhomboid muscle. There was a knot as old and as hard as a bitter memory. I paused, and then rotated over it slowly, as if through water. Her moan seemed to rise from a place deep inside her soul. It may have been a place she rarely visited.

Cantopop music from Hong Kong wafted from the adjoining kitchenette. Her two partially hidden colleagues were thumbing through Shanghai gossip magazines. They snuck glances at us in the foyer and choked back giggles to save for later.

'Now draw me,' demanded Dolly.

She stood up too quickly and suffered a head rush from the sudden drop in her blood pressure. I reached out to steady her with both hands on her shoulders. I held her until she brushed me away. She turned toward a window and drew the curtains apart. The late afternoon light flooded our space. She cracked open the double bay windows, hiked up her dress, and swung a coltish leg through the window. She posed, straddling the ledge.

'Draw.'

Her dangling foot swung puckishly back and forth. I sat in the chair again, picked up my journal and pencil, and placed them in my lap. I found my *Walkman*, snapped on my headphones, and pressed play. The voice of Prince singing *The Beautiful Ones* filled my ears. Staring at the light reflecting off her skin, I imagined how I would capture every detail: the edge of her mouth, the almond curve of her eyes, the proud but soft bridge of her nose, the minor constellation of beauty spots gathered near her left eye, the grace of her throat, the curl of her ear, the relaxed bend of her finger-tips, and the way her qipao dress hugged her waistline. I had no doubt she calculated how the afternoon light would bathe her body. Her intention may have been more than mere vanity. It felt closer to a celebration of beauty and play.

When we were finished, she climbed down from the window and smoothed out her dress. I stopped the music. I assumed she would be anxious to appraise my drawing of her. Instead, she held out her hand for my *Walkman.* I passed it over. She popped the tape and studied the label quizzically. Was she struggling to read English as well as she spoke it? Or perhaps she needed spectacles to read?

'My father spotted this *Walkman* on a TV commercial in Japan. He's been working over there. His secretary ordered one for me and one for him. It's the same metallic blue one used by the girl in the commercial he saw.'

I cringed when I remembered how I filled the air between us with things of no interest to anyone but me. Do you ever forgive the awkward and self-important teenager you left behind when you became an adult?

'I've a decent collection of cassettes at home. Drawing and music are everything to me. This *Walkman* is the latest *WM-101* with auto-reverse. It has a rechargeable gumstick battery...'

'Oh, I know all about the *Walkman*,' she interrupted as she handed it back to me and threw a wonderfully dismissive hand gesture.

She turned toward an ornate corner table and picked up a brocade handbag matching the color of her dress. She plucked out a Sony *WM-800 DUAL cassette* model *Walkman* released on the market at the same time as mine. The cassette on the red side of the unit would duplicate the cassette on the black side. If my *Walkman* was worth two weeks' salary in China, hers was worth three.

'How did you... I cannot even find these!'

She smiled a touch more than the Mona Lisa and brandished another nonchalant gesture with her hands.

'I'm a resourceful woman.'

'May I have a look at it?'

She placed it in my hand. I split each side in turn and discovered both cassettes were *TDK SA-X*. One cassette had "L Ronstadt" scrawled in approximated English characters. The other said "D Parton".

I reached into my jacket pocket and took out a blank cassette sealed in its gold wrapper. 'Here. I want you to have this. It's a 90-minute BASF *Chromdioxid Maxima*.' I put the cassette in her handbag. 'Chrome has a better signal-to-noise ratio.'

She did not seem to know what else to say except,

'Thank you.'

'You're most welcome.'

I returned her *Walkman* to her bag. There followed an awkward silence. She broke it with an insouciant offer.

'Well, if you want a massage after this, you have to pay, okay?'

In lieu of his affection, my father sent me an allowance I never spent. I may as well spend it at her parlor.

'Okay, I will. My name is David.'

Two

DOLLY

It was a strange day. It started out awful. I felt invisible again, like I don't matter. It took extra effort to see my own reflection resolve in the mirror. It was an image easily shattered with a single cruel word or gesture.

People told me I appeared strong. Appearances are the clothes we wear, the smile we pantomime. A smile is a mere muscle movement. How easily people are fooled! They wouldn't have recognised the frightened girl I was all those years ago. My life was interrupted. I'd missed important chapters in my history, and I was trying to rewrite my book. I needed help that was hard to find, and even harder to ask for in my world.

A customer told me today all of us Chinese girls look the same.

Fuck him.

Not fair! I never painted all white people with the same ugly brush. Surely there were good ones out there? On television there were good *gweilos*. I resigned myself to the awful truth that my parlor attracts only the worst of them.

These were some of the things that darkened my heart, so it was best to keep it hidden. I wouldn't want to bring another life into this world. I was glad I didn't have children. Not that I had a say in the matter. A doctor said I never will be a mother. Three miscarriages ruined my insides. A man once told me being infertile makes me a safe bet for a good screw.

Screw him.

Life can be both dark and light. If fortune favors me, then yin may follow yang. After the tourist fucked off, I let a pretty *gweilo* boy give me a massage. I told myself this was my birthday present to me. I turned 27 that day. I told no one, as usual. So long as no one knew the number, I could be any age I wanted. Most days I felt the same age as that boy.

He also drew sketches of me that took my breath away. Every detail of me was marked with the candid precision of a photo. He even included the details I don't like. He saw my flaws and continued to draw me until I was done. Each stroke of his pencil was made with a kind of unconditional affection. His complete and undiluted rendering of me made me feel beautiful. I felt seen. I felt like someone had walked into my bedroom, caught me naked, and I didn't mind at all. His drawing pulled me back into the world and made me feel like I was totally there.

I was too proud to let him know the extent of my delight. I'll admit I enjoyed watching him watching me as he drew me. His big round exotic green eyes stared at me, into me, with such frank absorption.

I loved that he was respectful enough not to idealize me. I hated the empty flattery of vanity portraits. I'd rather see the truth and find it wonderfully honest and therefore, honestly wonderful. There was one sketch in which he caught me biting my nails. It was a habit I couldn't quite shake. I was embarrassed at first, but he found the touching humanity in my silly compulsion. His drawings were more real than real.

Artists were reveling in realism at the time. I don't mean the big-name phonies who sleazed their way into government contracts. I'm talking about my friends who hosted modest exhibits in courtyards and teahouses. Their small audiences were growing in number and appetite. There was a well-seeded underground sprouting flowers of quiet truths rather than loud lies. Something exciting was happening in China. The future was an open question whispered between brushstrokes.

I was surprised to find this new realism in the white boy's drawings. The boy was a puzzle I wanted to solve. I'd never before heard a Caucasian speak in a perfect Szechuanese dialect. Although his grammar is far too formal. I'd never met a *gweilo* who grew up in my province. His clothing was amusing and, may I say, cute. There were beautiful boys wearing his clothes in American movies I enjoyed. Movies like *Weird Science* and *The Club for Breakfast*.

He tried to impress me with his tape player gadget. I enjoyed showing him that mine was bigger and more impressive. He was totally deflated. I didn't tell him a wealthy tourist left it behind when the bastard fled my parlor in haste. I don't know how much it cost, but it looked expensive. The boy was in love with my gadget. However, he thinks my tapes need chrome, or the signal ratio wasn't noisy enough, or something. Anyway, he gave me a brand-new cassette to use. It came in a gold wrapping so lovely I didn't want to open it. It was like a pretty mooncake you don't want to spoil by devouring it. I'd never had a fresh blank tape. I now had three tapes. Ha! He probably has a hundred, but so what?!

The other two girls gave me a hard time for the rest of the day. Lily and Cici would take turns making fun while they sipped hot tea from washed-out pickle jars. Throughout the day, they topped up their brew with boiled water from the three big flasks we kept in the kitchenette. Both girls visited the same hairdresser, and therefore they shared a matching Hong Kong style updo. That's where the similarity ended. Cici was the crazy one. She was never without a cigarette drooling from the corner of her mouth, one eye half closed against the wafting smoke. Lily was the quiet little sister. However, she wasn't so quiet on the day the white boy visited. Cici teased that I was a cradle-robber. Lily laughed uncontrollably while trying in vain to paint her nails. Her claws were famously long. Customers loved them. They were a shade of pink so bright it hurt your eyes. I laughed along with their taunts as I retreated into the dressing room where we got dolled up for the day.

We shared an old Hollywood-style dresser with a mirror bordered by lightbulbs. Some lights were brighter than others because the girls kept replacing dead bulbs with others of various wattages. There were pictures cut from contraband *Cosmopolitan* and *Vogue* magazines taped around the mirror's perimeter. Anyone could see I had a thing for American fashion models. My most cherished picture was a risqué photograph of Gia Carangi with her lover Sandy Linter. The image was totally raw sensuality. They were naked and separated only by a wire fence. The picture would be confiscated if ever I got raided. I took a seat on the shag carpet stool. I reached under the dresser where I keep my two secrets: my diary, and a pair of the thickest, ugliest glasses ever made. Nobody knew I needed them for reading. Lately I found myself digging through past entries while habitually chewing the nails of my left hand. I was scanning for clues that my life was not getting any better.

How was the boy intuitive enough to find the hard parts of me that needed massage? I must be a good teacher. Ha! My head felt light afterward, like smoking the first cigarette of the morning. If I were a hopeful person, I'd be entertaining naive thoughts that would be doomed from their inception. I never hope. Actually, I tell a lie. I never want to hope. Hope is Faith's richer, cruel sister.

Cici needed the dressing room. Luckily the girls knew to knock before they entered. I shoved my diary under the dresser with my awful glasses. Cici wandered in, trailing cigarette smoke like an acrid cape. She had to change into her army uniform she'd kept from her days in the reserves. Her special customer, Mister Huì, was visiting soon and he liked to do certain things that involved taking stern orders from her. She always looked forward to a big tip. We loved to listen through the thin walls and giggle at Cici reprimanding Mister Huì for crimes he committed that may or may not be true. Cici rummaged noisily in her wardrobe of clothes and things, spilling cigarette ash on everything. She wasn't finished gossiping about our young visitor.

'Lily said she'll date him if you don't have a try.'

'Who?'

I repainted my lips the deep *Shiseido* red used by the geisha of Kyoto.

'The white boy.'

'Oh yeah? She's certainly closer to his age than me.' I laughed and waved a dismissive hand.

I doubted he'd return to my parlor so I didn't bother remembering his name.

[illegible]asses. Cheyenne drew on, trailing cigarette smoke like [illegible]. She'd asked to change into her new uniform she'd [illegible] from her [illegible] in reserve. Her special customer, Master [illegible], was visiting soon and he liked to [illegible] that involved [illegible] from her. She [illegible]. We [illegible] through the [illegible] Mister [illegible] [illegible]

[illegible]

[illegible] I have a try.

[illegible]

[illegible] her lips [illegible] by the [illegible] K[illegible].

"The [illegible] he?"

[illegible] and [illegible].

I [illegible] the parlor [illegible].

Three

DAVID

I began visiting Dolly every Saturday afternoon. Although her parlor was close to my school, I refused to visit her on a weekday in my school uniform. I did not want her to see me as a kid. I wanted these visits to be something that existed outside of my childhood, to leave my juvenescence at the door when I climbed her staircase.

I always took my place in the same chair in front of the boudoir drawing from *Dream of the Red Chamber*. This was a story of a boy privileged with wealth and the affections of his many beautiful cousins. The cousin he chose to pursue was a frail and orphaned intellectual. Her name was Lin Daiyu. It was she who was in the drawing on the parlor wall. I would have felt less alone if I found a girl like Lin Daiyu. Somewhere out there was a girl who felt as orphaned as me. There were times I would arrive, and Dolly would be with another customer in one of three private rooms. Those rooms were darker than the rest of the parlor, save only for a soft scarlet light. Sometimes, when a door was cracked open wide enough, I could see a lamp shaded by a red silk scarf.

I was a spy in the house of ill repute. I was aware I was the only one who took the chair and not a private room. I was aware of *why* I was the only one in the chair and not a room. I was also canny enough to understand why there was no sign outside of her parlor. I was an old fifteen-year-old.

Her customers were mostly middle-aged men, sometimes older. One awkward younger customer left her parlor only a little less lost than when he arrived. None of these men were good looking. It made me wonder how numb you would have to be to touch someone intimately without even the slightest chemistry to coax you along. They came and went through her parlor in a bashful rush or inexplicable swagger. Occasionally I would try to sketch their comical demeanor in my art journals. This was how I dealt with my unusual situation.

When I wasn't drawing, I studied the lurid art-nouveau patterns in the rug under my feet. My favorite album to play on my *Walkman* while waiting was *The Head on the Door* by The Cure. Decades later, I would smile whenever I heard the naked whimsy of *In Between Days* or the manic confessional glee of *Close To Me.*

When she emerged from the darker room to greet me, our exchanges were quiet and decorous. I closed my eyes, shutting down one sense, amplifying the other four. I felt her pulse when she wrapped her palm across my forehead and slowly, firmly pressed her thumb under the occipital ridge at the back of my skull. There was a deep calm in the sound of her breathing. I savored the occasional soft smack of her lips as she chewed a stick of spearmint gum. The aggressively clean smell of lemon disinfectant throughout the parlor became associated in my mind with healing. I picked up every note from every torch song from the radio in the girls' kitchenette. The ballads of Anita Mui blended with the muted hum of the traffic outside.

It always amused Dolly when I returned her favor by massaging her in kind. I tried new moves she had tried on me. It was fun, like a peculiar dance. As I leaned into her shoulder, she understood this move required resistance from her. She dug her heels into the floor, pushed her back into me. I pressed my elbow into the space between her left rhomboid and her nape. Somewhere inside that space, I could feel a knot untie itself by degrees.

One day I left the parlor, stepped out onto the street, and the world smelled nicer than before. The air was still heavy, but I was buoyed by the humidity rather than drowned by it. The men blocking the sidewalk playing checkers no longer annoyed me. There were old ladies who stitched together pale yellow flowers and sold them on the street as perfume. It struck me as the most charming thing in the world on that day. This and other ordinary things intrigued me for the first time.

I walked home with this unnameable feeling. I found myself transfixed by the shadows made long by the sun falling low on the horizon. A ghost of a moon was rising. One by one, electric lights blinked on as twilight closed its hand over my city.

DOLLY

The boy turned up again the following Saturday afternoon. He was wearing a white tee-shirt. His jeans looked like they'd been washed in bleach. The shoulders of his matching jacket were totally too big. Was he on his way to a date? I'd forgotten his name after all. Thank goodness he introduced himself again.

'Remember me? My name is David. I visited you last Saturday.'

Of course I'd remember the only customer whose face didn't look as bad as they smell.

He sat in the chair. I took a longer time than what's appropriate to tie his hair back. I hadn't touched *gweilo* hair like his before. It draped in my hands like blonde silk. What conditioner did he use?

As my thumbs dug into the sides of his throat, there was none of the fight-or-flight tension that I felt from most customers. I was surprised by how much he surrendered to me even when I applied the hardest pressure. I wished I trusted others so easily.

He always closed his eyes when I touched him. This was lucky for me. He never caught me watching him. His crazy long lashes fanned out under his closed eyelids. Why are white boys lucky with lashes for fucks' sake? His nose was quite beautiful as well. His profile was as striking as one of those bronze figures sculpted by Rodin. I am sure he makes all the little girls at school wet themselves.

Once again, he spent the last half of our session massaging my old knots. He was becoming more expert with every visit. Perhaps he was practicing with his family? The girls at work practiced on me, but they couldn't discover my pain like he could. His hair occasionally brushed my skin. At first, it tickled. Eventually I relaxed and it was... pleasant.

Anyway, the boss was giving me a hard time again. Fatty Dong accused me of stealing from him. He visited my parlor unannounced as usual. He enjoyed irritating us working girls. He was probably one of those grubby boys in school who snapped bra straps because that's the closest he could hope to get to a girl. One could always tell when he was pleased with himself by the way he played with his balls. Fatty liked to roll two metal Baoding balls between his fingers whenever discussing business. The metal balls would clang obnoxiously against the stupid number of rings on his fingers. In theory, Baoding balls were used for medicinal purposes. In practice, they were favored by short, ugly, self-important men who wanted to pretend they were badass. A smug satisfaction spread across his porcine face as he scolded me.

'I've watchers who count how many customers enter this parlor and it doesn't reflect on the books, my dear.'

'Then your watchers need to go back to school and learn how to count.'

I popped a stick of *Yiqing* spearmint gum into my mouth and chewed while I stared into his dead piggy eyes. I was bored with crude men who acted like they were more clever than me.

DAVID

I felt envious of everyone else in China who had the option to adopt a Western name. I already had a Western name and it never occurred to anyone that I should adopt a Mandarin name. What fun it would be to carry an extra name in your pocket! One could reinvent themselves, armed with a second name, like a second face.

Dolly wanted to show me why she chose her Western name. After one of our Saturday afternoon sessions, she invited me out with Lily and Cici to a late night Karaoke bar. She knew I could not resist anything related to music. The two younger girls were elated and giggly beyond my understanding at the time. We left the parlor in high spirits and walked the six blocks to *Okey Dokey Videoke*.

The late nights of Chengdu were sleepy, but alert with one eye open. Scattered shopfronts kept their lights on, even if it were only a single bulb that burned. Their keepers lounged on chairs facing the sidewalk, smoking cigarettes in that sideways fashion only Chinese people can do. There was always a small dog or cat on the step keeping a lazy watch on the foot traffic. Like their owners, their gaze was fixed on the middle distance, waiting for something to happen.

We passed a rickshaw driver taking a rest sitting in his carriage, a grandma selling rich fragrant *Mapo tofu*, and a bicycle repairman covered in chain oil and road grime. All three of them stared at our colorful gang-of-four painted on a monochrome canvas. In a city heavy with half-finished buildings and half-hearted hopes, we were the only things that appeared complete.

The façade of *Okey Dokey Videoke* was built around a giant plastic foam semi-quaver. Dolly negotiated some kind of transaction with the cashier girl. She led us down a tight hallway and into a dark, teak-paneled room filled with the cigarette fog from the last group of patrons. Apparently, that was still not quite enough smoke because Cici lit up three cigarettes and passed two to the other girls. The cashier girl returned bearing four bottles of *Tsingtao* beer and a cast iron hot plate stacked with skewered barbecued eggplant. She laid out the feast on a low table built from an old door. Cici snapped off the tops of the bottles and passed them around. No one seemed too concerned I was only 15. Lily was not much older than I. China is like that.

Dolly tapped instructions into the Laserdisc karaoke machine. With a glint in her eye I had never seen before, she set up a track and grabbed a microphone. The monitor burst into life. The song began with a rousing piano intro, backed up by a typewriter rhythm section, no less.

Dolly launched the first verse of *9 to 5*. My mouth hung open in astonishment as perfect American English words poured from the mouth of a Chengdu girl. Her singing voice was made more surreal by the southern twang she curled around the edge of the lyrics. The girls squealed in delight like their team kicked a goal. Cici threw down the skewer she was devouring and grabbed the other two microphones for herself and Lily. They followed the monitor, anticipating the big chorus. Propelled by an infectious, stomping rhythm, the big chorus moment arrived, and all three girls belted out the words. The toll of their working week was unloaded into this crowded little box. The girls purged something beyond my limited understanding. Their anthem ended and they clanged their beer bottles together like the unruly frat boys I saw in American films.

I wanted in on the fun. The pale lager in my bloodstream gave me some Dutch courage. I thought of a song I enjoyed singing in the shower while daydreaming of a duet with someone. I stepped up to the machine. With a little help from Dolly, I found the track I wanted named after a Hemingway novel. She instantly recognised *Islands in the Stream*.

She asked eagerly, 'Can I sing this one with you?'

'I would be honored', I replied with a pantomimed gentility.

The three girls gasped as I sang the opening verse. Dolly sang the next and claimed it as her own. When it was my turn, I replied to her call. Together, we shared the harmony of the chorus. I gazed at Dolly in awe from the first word she sang until the last. She matched the tender joy of her namesake. We stole looks at each other whenever we were not following the monitor. The song was a dance of two voices trying on roles. It was a four-minute and eight-second chance to see how the role may fit.

In the wake of our song, there was a pregnant pause filled with unsaid things. Our eyes darted all over the room except at each other. We broke the tension by chatting about how Western pop music helped us both to speak English. Meanwhile, the other two girls whispered secret things into each other's eager ears.

DOLLY

David visited again today for our Saturday afternoon booking. He was the rare customer who used the chair. Most preferred a private room, but I won't have him there. Cici once threatened to take him into her room if he ever arrived in my absence. She lit a *Lesser Panda* cigarette.

'One hour with me and he'll forget all about his Dolly.'

I smacked her cheeky ass.

I looked forward to his visits... begrudgingly. A fresh face is always welcome when you work in a stale job. I enjoyed the way he talked about Western pop music. He spoke in depth about singers I didn't know, but I pretended I knew anyway. Days later, I asked my bootleg music friend to find me songs by some white lady named Pat Benatar. David illustrated his feelings about music with the most curious words nobody else used. He described songs using line and shade as if sketching it all out in those books he carried. His strokes were delicate or bold, and sometimes blended with the palm of his hand. Am I talking about his words, his drawings, or the way he rubs me the right way, for fucks' sake?!

He was a tall boy. When he stood before me, I looked up to him, and my eyes did funny things. That's all I'll say about that.

Because he was a tall bastard, I brought in a wooden box for me to step up. From my higher position, I was able to totally hammer down into his shoulders. The box was only for him.

When it was his turn to massage me, I tried closing my eyes like he did. I quickly understood why he enjoyed being blind. All of my other senses were dialed up. I smelled the familiar buttery soap of his shampoo. I was certain the brand was *Fabergé*, the kind with wheat germ oil and honey. I hadn't been able to find it in the shops anymore. He must've been spoiled with connections I didn't have. In the darkness under my eyelids, my ears pricked at the rhythm of his breathing. It was long and deep.

He gently untied my hair and combed it out with his fingers, letting me know he was finished with me. I was left feeling a kind of manic hunger. I was craving some barbecue and singing. I decided we're all going out for karaoke. The girls and I serviced a few more customers while David waited—he's a patient boy. We then locked up and hit the street. My favorite karaoke joint was only five blocks away. Everyone on the street stared at the three parlor girls leading the blonde boy astray.

Turned out David was quite good at karaoke! We all appreciated having a male voice in the mix. I imagined he practiced a lot in the shower. He looked at me when he sang and rarely needed the words on the screen. He made me feel every lyric of the song as if I were hearing the words for the first time.

We drank a lot, especially me. I paid for it with a splitting headache the next day at work.

'There must be more to life than drowning it in beer?'

'If you find out what it is, let me know. I want some of that,' Cici quipped as she lit a cigarette off the embers of her last one.

Lily offered me aspirin from her big pink faux fur purse. How did she know I was suffering a headache? It was not the first time this young girl showed sensitivity beyond her years.

'Thank you, darling.'

'Do you want me to rub your temples?'

'Yes, please. I'll owe you one.'

I sat in David's chair, snapped open my big man-sized folding fan and cooled my neck. Lily pressed her fingers across my brow-line in slow, deliberate points of pressure.

Cici cried out, 'Travel!'

'What about travel?' I asked.

'Travel is something "more to life". If I could travel, I'd visit Rome.'

'What would you do in Rome, dreamer? Dance in a fountain, probably.'

Lily giggled. Cici drew deeply on her cigarette, blew a perfect ring of smoke and contemplated.

'Actually, I'd sit at one of those alfresco cafes. I'd wear big dark sunglasses, sip espresso, and watch the nuns walk by.'

'You don't even like coffee, Cici. Why the dark sunglasses?'

'Big dark sunglasses is what Audrey Hepburn wore, in the *Tiffany Breakfast* movie!'

Everyone burst into laughter. I almost fell out of David's chair. Eventually, Lily gained back control of my head and returned to cradling my temples in her expert hands.

Cici had more to say.

'Audrey's sunglasses were made by Oliver Goldsmith. They're the best ones. The frames appear black, but they're actually a rich tortoiseshell color. Her lenses are deep crystal green so dark that nobody can catch her eyes. Nobody knows her true feelings.'

'What would happen if someone knew what she was feeling?' I asked.

'Audrey can't let that happen. She needs everyone to think she's the crazy party girl and nothing more. She protects herself.'

Lily waited for a beat of silence before she shared her thoughts with us.

'I want to ride a stallion in Spain.'

The soft tones of her voice carried a self-assured conviction.

'A horse?' asked Cici.

'A stallion... in Spain. The southern peninsula of Spain is called Andalusia. It's a wilder part of the country. There were monks who bred the world's finest horses hundreds of years ago. The Andalusian horse is more sensitive and beautiful than other breeds. His mane and tail are longer and thicker. He's athletic, a controlled power. I dream about riding fast against the wind. The Sierra Madre in my sight.'

I said, 'That's beautiful, Lily.'

'My massage or my dream?'

'Both.'

We shared a smile.

Cici announced, 'It's your turn, Dolly. Where would you go? What would you do?'

My answer surprised all of us.

'I want to be buried in a land with a bright blue sky. I want to live out my last days in a country where the colors pop so bright they hurt your eyes.'

DAVID

Dolly faced the wall in the parlor chair in front of me. Her hands relaxed in her lap. Her eyes closed like last time. A vast reserve of trust is involved when you let someone touch you with your eyes closed. I wrapped the palm of my hand across her forehead. Then I pressed my thumb under the occipital ridge at the back of her skull. This was the move she used on me to drown out a headache. I felt Dolly let go of something intangible inside her. Her hands fell to her sides as if she were a marionette and the wires that controlled her were cut away.

She said quietly, 'I could have used this after our night at *Videoke* last week.'

Her quiet words were still clear enough for the girls to hear. They always seemed eager to listen in on my visits.

Cici cried out from the kitchenette, 'Come out with us again tonight, David!'

Late into the evening, we found ourselves inside another karaoke room. Our table was soon lavished with Chengdu snacks called *guo kui*. The house cook rolled out a tender dough, twice-stuffed with spiced ground beef. He then folded the mix into perfect palm-sized pancakes, deep-fried until golden, and then baked in a smoky charcoal pit. When you bite into the flaky crispy pastry, the oozing liquid fills your mouth with a delicious fire. It was worth spilling flakes of pastry all over ourselves. We washed down these snacks with a couple of rounds of *Tsingtao* lager.

This time, Lily and Cici took over the karaoke machine. They plugged in their requests and sang Alan Tam songs until there was no more of him left on the laserdisc.

Dolly took her cue to enter a song request of her own. She plucked two mics from the table and gave one to me. As soon as the track title lit up on the monitor, I knew that she knew the song was right for me. I showed everyone I was more than familiar with the lyrics of *We've Got Tonight*. The song was an open hand held out from one lonely heart to another. When it was Dolly's verse, she did not need the words on the monitor. She must have practiced her verses. She looked straight at me and sang about a search that she was longing to end. We slipped into the costume of the song for a few minutes to see how these roles may fit. It was a chance to ponder a caution thrown to the wind of the music.

After karaoke sessions, we enjoyed a little tradition of walking home together in the fresh air. It was the perfect way to tie off the evening. There was always the odd food or drink stand open in the small hours. On a sultry night of too much singing, our throats were parched. Not far from the bars, there was a popular iced tea cart owned by the Bau brothers. The two boys always shared a joke or some local gossip. Their teas were brewed with freshly picked leaves and not concentrates nor powders. Dolly always chose a tall cup of peach oolong with pearls made from the starch of cassava root.

We strolled past the shuttered shops and lit windows of cozy terraced homes. The only traffic was a grocer riding her tricycle laden with unsold fruit. Her infant sat in a box among the apples and oranges happily chatting with her mother as she peddled home. Bugs swarmed under the warm glow of the sodium-vapor streetlamps while we chatted about things uttered only late at night. Cici was pining for the man she met before her husband.

'I miss my Hūan. Don't you guys dare tell my husband! Hūan was like the perfect hotpot... a blend of sweet and spicy. We should have run away together. Screw my parents.'

She dropped her cigarette on the ground, smeared it under her heel, and lit up another.

Lily giggled.

'You're so crazy.'

'Am I crazy to love him? Maybe. I still love him. There. I said it. I don't care if I bring trouble.'

'I want to say something too,' Lily declared and paused for dramatic effect.

'I fell for one of our customers. Remember the young public servant?'

A sad, knowing smile curled the edge of Dolly's mouth.

'The government relocated him to Shanxi, yes?'

'Yes. 1320 kilometers away, and I'm sad. I never told him my feelings. Now it's too late'

Lily stared at her shoes.

Dolly had a gift for finding the perfect words to pull Lily from her sulk.

'Watch and wait. If you were meant to be together, the clouds will part, and fate will bring him back to you. Though he may be a thousand miles away, trust in *Yuánfèn* (fate). He'll find you again.

Lily exhaled deeply and cast a smile in Dolly's direction. Cici slung her arm around Lily's shoulders.

I envied the palpable sense of trust and intimacy within this triumvirate of friends. I had the urge to share something that was weighing on me. I confessed I suffered from nightmares, reliving my mother's death. Lily and Cici gasped in sympathy. Dolly took a thoughtful sip from her tea.

'You know, I could feel something was not quite right with you today.'

'Her obituary said her heart failed. Truth is, no one knows why she died, only what she died from. Something went wrong with her heart, probably days before she fell. She didn't trust Chinese doctors. She refused to go to the hospital. I remember the date—December 8th, 1980. A delivery man came to our Beijing apartment. He found her disoriented. Ma was trying to say something.

She collapsed in the hallway. Never woke up. My father dealt with his pain by moving. That's how we landed in Chengdu. It wasn't long before he rebounded into Mei Mei. They married quickly. It was like a hasty tourniquet to stop a wound from bleeding.'

Lily and Cici gushed words of compassion, while Dolly fell into a cool, stunned silence.

We arrived first at Cici's home where she lived with her husband. He did not meet her at the door. However, she was welcomed home by Winston, her two-year-old Shar-Pei dog.

Three blocks further on was Dolly's flat. It was an art-deco walk-up above a Go chess school. The Master was often tutoring a student deep into the night. Dolly knew him by name. He waved to her through his window. His little school was lit by a single tungsten bulb. His eyes were gentle and always watching, even when they were not.

The last girl to escort home was Lily. She lived with her parents and two older sisters. She was born before the one-child policy, so she got to enjoy the company of siblings who adored her (for good reason). It was her habit to become shy when it was only the two of us. Her face flushed pink and she managed to say,

'I'm sorry about your mother, David.'

The front entry light of her neat little home blinked on. One of her sisters cracked open the screen door for her.

'Thank you,' I said. 'See you next Saturday afternoon.'

DOLLY

David was in my chair again yesterday. I discovered something hard on the left side of his neck. I wrapped my hand around the right side of his head and pushed the palm of my other hand into the hardness. With a circular movement, I pressed into the knot and felt it release after a while. What was weighing on him, for fucks' sake? He had nothing to complain about. That *gweilo* may have grown up here, but he lived the comfortable life of a wealthy foreigner. The Dan-Dan noodle soup man on the street needed a rub down more than this kid. Let's see how long the boy would last lugging a pole across his shoulders all day with a bucket of soup on either end. His shoulders may look strong, but I doubt he'd last five minutes. Anyway, I was glad I healed the knot in his pampered broad shoulders.

Fatty Dong came by later to say sorry for giving me a hard time about the books. He fidgeted with his beloved Baoding balls behind his back. I accepted his apology with grace he didn't deserve. I was glad my friend in the State Tax Administration told Dong to back off. Sometimes good fortune smiles on me.

The girls wanted to invite David to karaoke again. I agreed so long as they behaved and didn't embarrass themselves by acting like horny teenage girls. I'm glad they asked because I'd chosen the perfect song for David seeing as he liked that bearded country singer so much.

I discovered more about this boy. His family is broken. I suspected he had yet to discover the full extent of the damage. I wondered if his father found a Japanese girlfriend? I doubted he'd return for his son. There were too many men like this. I didn't want to think about it anymore. Who was this poor rich boy to me anyway?

DAVID

1986 was the year of the Tiger. The only way to describe Chinese New Year to a foreigner is to imagine the familial togetherness of Christmas and smash it together with the bacchanalian excess of the western New Year's Eve. The festivities span twenty-three days, ending on the fifteenth night of the first lunar month of the Chinese calendar. This night is known as the

Festival of Lanterns. That was the year the parlor girls and I ventured out onto the streets to see the sky fill with lanterns of every shade of red.

Our gang-of-four wandered among the throng while eating *Tang You Guo Zi*—skewers of sweet deep-fried sticky rice balls rolled in toasted sesame seeds. All the eateries remained open for trade. Every thoroughfare was filled with people who were hungry, thirsty, and jubilant. There was pop music up ahead. We found ourselves drawn to it as if by collective inertia. The infectious beats and joyous Western vocals were coming from a hefty crowd of teenage revellers. I discerned the familiar sound of Wham! singing *I'm Your Man* from a Hi-Fi somewhere (This pop duo broke ground in China by touring Beijing the previous year).

The ebb and flow of the crowd grew less manageable the deeper we sunk into the mass of bodies. Dolly and I lost the girls in the human riptide and found ourselves locked in a cozy enclave of young people dancing—mimicking moves borrowed from bootleg clips from MTV.

The music switched suddenly to the gentle opening strains of a familiar Hollywood love theme. We looked at one another and shared a momentary awkwardness that melted into something else. We were out of view from anyone who knew us. Dolly and I were alone with a ballad that had the power to slow down the body but not the heart. The music was treacly sweet and naive, but the yearning was so raw that it hurt. Our arms slipped all too easily around each other's bodies. We blended into the crowd of first-time young lovers. I whispered the opening lyrics of *Almost Paradise* into her ear. She answered by whispering the next verse into mine. I felt a rush through my body that began with her words that all her life she only needed me.

The ballad ended too soon as the word spread like wildfire it was time to release the lanterns. The crowd dispersed in the direction of The People's Park and we followed.

Revellers filled the space, trying in earnest to launch their delicate red paper lanterns by lighting the small candle within. Soon the sky became the world's most elegant fire hazard. I felt as if I was rudely awoken from one daydream only to find myself in another.

DOLLY

Last night I enjoyed a waking dream. I dreamt I'd never been exiled as a teenager to the country by the government. I dreamt I was at my formal school dance that never happened. I imagined dancing slow with my beau. The place was filled with couples as if it were a hall of mirrors, infinite reflections of pairs upon pairs of young lovers. The crowd closed the space between David and I. Sixteen-year-old white boys are tall for their age. I stepped my feet up onto his. When he moved in circles to the music, I moved with him. My arms slid second-nature around the tight drum of his body. My right hand found purchase under his shirt and smoothed across the warm skin of his back. I looked up and saw my reflection in his jade-fire eyes. He never knew the teenage me. Would he have danced with me with my hair hacked short like all the other girls at the labour farms? Would he have danced with me in those shapeless dungarees they made us wear?

I was feeling my age because two lines appeared at the corners of my eyes where there used to be none. He helped me forget those lines for a while. I turned 28 that day. As usual, I didn't tell a soul.

DAVID

Mei Mei preferred that I escort her when she shopped for produce at the bustling Sunday markets. I suspected she enjoyed people looking at us when we walked together. I did not mind obliging her vanity if it made her happy. Besides, she needed help carrying everything back home.

I enjoyed indulging in the intoxicating color and aroma of the market. There were mountains of fiery red chillies, pickled preserves, and pungent homemade sauces. Giant watermelons filled the tray-back of a 1960s *Jiefeng* army truck. Some were cut open to reveal the rich red fruit inside. A family of farmers from the country sold plump tomatoes that were ripe and fleshy. It was all too tempting to pick one up and gorge yourself. I looked forward to the smell of barbecue skewers and roasted red peppers cooking on makeshift charcoal grills. Mei Mei had a penchant for crunchy spring rolls filled with leafy vegetables and red oil.

We loved *Zhangji* strawberries, but for more than a year they had disappeared from the market. On the rare occasion we found a punnet, they were terribly overpriced. Government ministers were staking out a lucrative monopoly on certain produce and wholesaling their stock at criminally high prices.

Min was our favorite fruit vendor. One day she told us she saved a gift for us. She presented us with a punnet of the freshest strawberries. She said the punnet was free, and we should be expecting one every Sunday.

'Someone is taking care of you.'

Mei Mei was delirious with gratitude. She demanded to know the identity of our benefactor. Min said our guardian angel wished to remain anonymous.

As if on cue, I spied Dolly in a sapphire blue qipao dress wandering with elegant ease through the labyrinthine market. Her hair was folded into a graceful side-bun. She bore a basket of lychees in one hand and a tall plastic cup of iced tea in the other. She was wired for sound with her headphones snapped on and her DUAL cassette *Walkman* fixed to her hip. The bold clash of old and new fashion drew stares from fellow shoppers. She disappeared into the crowd as if she were a trick my mind played on me.

DOLLY

I always ate my lunch at a street food stand that served the best *Tian Shui Mian* (sweet water noodles). I sat on an unsteady stool at the rough counter. My back was only inches from passing bicycles. The guy who ran the joint was Jiang. He'd been doing this since he was old enough to work. His economy of movement was so smooth he never broke a sweat while cooking and serving solo. I found it relaxing watching him make my meal. He lifted a few skeins of freshly kneaded noodles from a big pot of boiling water and dropped them into my soup bowl. The thick noodles resembled uneven ropes and lay steaming, waiting for the sauce. Into a smaller porcelain bowl, he trickled red soy sauce, a dab of crushed garlic, a spray of fresh roasted Szechuan peppercorns, a dash of sesame paste, and finally a darkly rich chili oil blended from his secret family recipe. The mixture was whisked with chopsticks and drizzled over the noodles. The final touch was a generous sprinkling of coarse flakes of sugar.

When I used my own chopsticks to mix the noodles with the sauce, each strand came alive as it was coated with flavor. Every bite I took burst in my mouth with sweetness and prickling spiciness. Jiang's *Tian Shui Mian* was my favorite comfort food to ward off the blues.

I paid him with my unfurled notes, and he kept the change as usual.

'Something not right today, Dolly?'

He busied himself rolling fresh dough across his floured board, one eye alert for my reply.

'Fatty Dong is on my back about the business again, Jiang. That's all'. He pondered this for a moment.

'Is it?'

'Is what?'

'Is that all?'

'No.'

I wished I'd told him more. This quagmire I'd stepped in has made me the lonely person who can't share her pain. There was not one person in the country who understood why I felt this way toward someone I shouldn't.

I tried in vain to follow the threads of my past to something that would justify all this silly melancholy. I'd nothing to compare my current state of affairs. I recalled several lovers who stood out for reasons both good and ultimately bad. I dated a magazine editor named Zhāng who confessed an undying affection for me until the day I met his parents. There was also a man named Liú. I met him every morning at the same time at the same bakery until one day I asked him to have tea with me. I believe my forward move may have startled the poor guy. I don't think he appreciated a woman taking the initiative. It showed in the bedroom when his arousal was not forthcoming. On the other hand, Lingyun's cock was as ready and reliable as a loyal soldier. I met him when he was an ambitious bureaucrat. This I was willing to tolerate because he was as handsome as the devil. One day he told me two pieces of news: he was being promoted in the ranks of the Communist Party; and he was leaving town and couldn't see me anymore. A month later I caught him having dinner at a particularly good wonton restaurant with another woman. He hadn't moved to another city. He'd merely moved down the street to another woman's house. She was a nice woman who didn't work in a parlor. She'd make a good public wife. I asked her if Lingyun still enjoyed wearing a brassiere while he fucked. That got the attention of everyone in the restaurant. I left him, the restaurant, and the unpleasantness behind. No man would be the weather in my sky, unless that weather was clear.

My experience with men was that they listened far too much to the voices of others, or worse, the stupid voices in their heads. David seemed to defy these voices. Was it because he was young? Fuck, he was so young!

I finished my lunch. My body radiated with goodness. Jiang offered me a warm smile as I left his stand. His company and his noodles made me feel a little less alone.

DAVID

More than a year passed, and I could not imagine a Saturday afternoon without her company. The girls and I would often spend the evening enjoying hot pot or karaoke. Although there were four of us, there were moments when it felt like there was only two of us. Dolly gave me her phone number in case I ever needed to cancel a massage. I never called to cancel.

Soon it was summer, which cooled into Autumn. This was the season of our moon festival. The event falls on the fifteenth day of the eighth lunar month in the Chinese calendar. The moon is the fullest and brightest that evening.

Mei Mei was celebrating with her family. Every year they played mah-jong and ate every moon-shaped food known to Szechuan cuisine. I was alone at home with the faraway noise of people gathering and merging into a single hum. Someone in our street was playing long, bright wistful notes of joy on a traditional dizi, a 9000-year-old bamboo flute. I turned off all the lights in the apartment. The only light remaining was from the moon outside the big living room window that refused to open.

I took Dolly's number from my wallet and stared at it for ages hoping it would ring itself so I would not need to. Our phone was an American rotary-dial Bell Western *Electric 554* bolted to the living room wall. Mei Mei refused to upgrade to a keypad model because the Bell Western was such a lovely shade of coral pink. Its long curly cord suited my habit of striding around the apartment while talking on the phone. However, I lacked the confidence to stride that night. After I dialed her number, I put the receiver to my ear, pushed my back to the wall, slid to the floor, and waited for her to pick up. Why would she be home? Surely, she would be out there celebrating. Why would she be as alone as I am?

And yet, she picked up my call.

'Hello?'

'It's David. I didn't expect you to answer.'

'Why call me then?' followed by a playful little laugh.

The telephone amplified every nuance in her voice. The inflections at the ends of her words were now writ large. It was like hearing my favorite song remastered. I wished I had something more clever to say.

'The moon is particularly beautiful this year. What do you think?'

There was a pause. If she were flippant again, I would have to answer her banter. I am shit at banter. I wanted her to meet me in a serious place.

'Yes. It is beautiful.'

Yes!

'Turn off all your lights. The moon fills your home with its glow if you do that.'

'I already have, David.'

Say my name again.

'David, did your school teach you the words to the poem, *Water Melody* by Su Shi? It's from the Song Dynasty.'

'Yes. *When will the moon be clear and bright? With a cup of wine in my hand, I ask the clear sky...*'

She jumped ahead in the poem, and honeyed her voice a little more than usual.

'I want to ride the wind to fly home.

I fear the crystal and jade mansions

Much too high and cold for me...'

I broke in to recite the next stanza.

'Dancing with my moonlit shadow.

It does not seem like the human world...'

Again, she skipped ahead.

'...Why does the moon tend to be full when people are apart?'

This time I skipped to the final words.

'...Though a thousand miles apart, we are still able to share the beauty of the moon together.'

'Sweet dreams, *qīnài de*.'

Click.

'Good night, Dolly,' I whispered into the dead phone line.

Qīnài de is a term of endearment reserved for lovers and the beloved.

DOLLY

David's voice on the telephone—mmm.

Not long after I answered his call, I spread the lips of my pussy wide with the fingers of my left hand while I slowly teased my clit with the fingertips of my right. It began as an idle pleasure. However, by the time he was speaking of moonlit shadows or whatever, my fingers were whirring over my engorged clit. I kept dipping my fingers into my wet pussy for lubrication. The trickiest part was cradling my phone between my ear and my shoulder. Not to mention the struggle to sound sensible to this poor boy who was only trying to have a decent conversation with me. How would he feel about me if he knew what I was doing? What if I told him I was playing with myself? The idea caused a feeling of molten lava to grow in my tummy. I hung up on him before I did something naughty and confessed everything. My orgasm hit me like a truck. It was like my body was being rude to me for thinking such things. Exhausted,

I sprawled across my double bed damp with sweat and stared at the growing crack in my ceiling.

DAVID

Dolly ended our call abruptly. I wondered if she was upset about something.

Qīnài de.

Her voice kept rewinding and playing back in my head. Until that phone call, I had no idea a collection of sentences could carry so much heat. It was not the words she said that burned me up, but the intonation of each syllable from her mouth. I needed to cool down and decompress. I tore off my clothes and slid into bed without bothering to put on pajamas. I was hot.

The cold hard light of the moon flooded my window like a midnight sun. The strange light forced a fresh perspective on my room. There were drawings taped to every available surface except for the space on the wall above my bed. A cheval mirror stood in a corner. It reflected an image of me lying below a void. I felt an urgent need to fill that space.

My nerves were so raw that I was startled out of bed by the sharp crack of high heels outside our door. Mei Mei was home. Her keys jangled for far too long in the lock. She must have gotten sloppy drunk with her family. My suspicion was confirmed when her keys crashed to the floor. I went to the linen closet, grabbed a fresh towel, wrapped it around my waist, and opened the door for my stepmother.

Despite her intoxication, she tossed her keyring with practiced precision into the small porcelain bowl by the door. She fell into my arms and pressed her cheek to my bare chest. Her voice slurred.

'You're so warm.'

I held her tight and kicked the door shut behind her. She reeked of baijiu liquor and about a hundred cigarettes. Her beautiful lavender chiffon dress needed dry-cleaning. The dress was tailored to her body and was one of her favorites. I would take it to *Mr Tan's Laundromat* first thing in the morning. I picked up her pink suede handbag where it fell from her fingers and placed it on a side table. She needed help stepping out of her matching heels. Later, I would place them in their original box for her. My immediate concern was to ensure she was safe and sound in bed. I tried to guide her in that direction, but she seemed a little too dazed to decide what to do next. Taking the initiative, I did something I could do now I was no longer the little boy she met years ago. I scooped her up into my arms and carried her down the hall. A grin spread across her face as I literally swept her off her feet. She was even lighter than she looked. I imagined carrying a child.

'Let's get you to bed, young lady.'

Her brow furrowed.

'I need to pee first.'

I stopped short of her room, backed up to the bathroom, and set her down carefully next to the toilet. I left the room and closed the door behind me as she hiked up her dress.

Standing in the hallway, I listened for tell-tale signs she was okay. My mind wandered. I rewound Dolly's voice in my head.

Why does the moon tend to be full when people are apart?

So full.

I discovered my cock had grown hard underneath my bath towel. I could not recall when it began, but there it was, pointing straight up like a flagpole. It was firm and fat against the towel wrapped tight against my body. My cock pulsed and bucked against the fabric, wanting out. There was a feeling of water building up against a dam.

I heard Mei Mei flush the toilet. In China, in those days, flushing meant pouring a bucket of water into the bowl. I knocked on the door.

'Are you okay?'

Silence.

'Ma?'

'Yes?'

'May I come in?'

'Yes.'

As I opened the bathroom door, I caught her throwing her underwear across the bathroom into the laundry bin. Again, her aim was eerily deft despite her inebriated state. Wearing a playful grin, she raised her arms.

'Pick me up again?'

'Oh, you like that? Okay, Miss.'

I lifted her up and cradled her in my arms. She buried her face into the arch of my neck. I made my way slowly to her bedroom. I was worried moving too fast would make her sick. She slipped out of my arms and leaned against me as I parted her linen and helped her slide under her sheet. I left her curled up in a fetal position with a smile on her face and her eyes yet to close.

I was still hot.

I returned to the bathroom, shed my towel to release my cock from confinement, and blasted my body with a cold shower until I could not stand it anymore. I turned off the water and listened to the drops fall away from me onto the tiles. The air felt crisp on my skin as it dried. My body cooled, but my cock remained hot and hard. So much for the theory that a cold shower cools your libido—quite the opposite. The shock of the icy water seemed to have fired up every nerve ending. I walked naked back to bed.

I was mentally exhausted but physically wide awake. The moonlight through my window defined the contours of my cock pressed under my bed sheet. I marveled at how it kicked against the linen when I tensed the muscles in my pelvis. Our summer linen was seriously thin so that every topographic detail of my body was in sharp relief against the almost sheer fabric. My legs stretched out almost too long for that old double bed. My thighs clenched tight. Every muscle in my legs popped. I ran the tip of my index finger from the base of my shaft along the length up to my head and pressed the soft sensitive flesh there. I let it go, engaged my pelvic muscle again. My cock rose and made a tent of my bed sheet. My tummy undulated at the sensation of rubbing myself against the fabric.

That was when Mei Mei walked into my bedroom.

She sat on my bed beside the tent I erected. I assumed she was too drunk to notice it right away. She had changed out of her dress and into her pale peach silk chemise. Her bum was pressed up against my hip. She had brushed her teeth. I could smell the fresh mint flavor of toothpaste when she spoke in broken unsteady thoughts.

'Do you ever think... do you ever get... lonely?'

I had so much to say about that, but I kept my answer brief.

'Yes. I am lonely most of the time, but I'm beginning to know what not being lonely feels like.'

'I can stay home more if you want me to, I can...'

'No. It's okay.'

The moon bathed her in a melancholy light and cast dark shadows over her eyes.

'I don't want you to feel...'

She was struggling with something. Her brow furrowed as she absently rubbed my tummy like she used to when I was younger. Back then, she joked that I was her happy little Buddha and she rubbed my tummy for luck. That seemed so long ago. My tummy had become quite sleek since those days, and there was no more baby fat for her to rub. Now her hands were gliding perilously close to my painfully hard cock.

'I don't want you to feel like I'll leave you like... like... they did... your mother and father.'

Her high voice pitched even higher as if she were worried I could not hear her intent.

'I know you won't do that.'

'I won't leave you.'

What else do you say when someone makes such a promise?

'I know, Ma.'

She looked at me and sighed deeply from the effort it took to be understood. Then her hand swept across my shaft, which caused me to make a tent again. Her eyes grew the size of pork buns as they fell upon my cock. We both froze. Her mouth made the shape of...

'Oh.'

...and stayed that way for the longest moment. I broke the tension first.

'I'm sorry.'

I had no idea why I was apologizing, but it seemed to be contagious.

'No, *I'm* sorry.'

She kept looking at my cock as if she suddenly discovered I was holding a puppy in my lap and she thought it was the cutest thing.

'Well, it's been awhile since I've seen... *bǎo bèi*.'

The term *bǎo bèi* means baby, or treasured object. This is what she named it when we would shower together in the early days after she married my father. The official reason was that we were saving water. However, our showers also served as a peculiar bonding time.

She cooed over her treasured object.

'Hello, *bǎo bèi*.'

I let a chuckle escape me. Why did she have to give it a name?! She grinned while she pressed the skin on either side of the base of my cock and watched it stand up tall underneath my sheet. I felt opposing compulsions fight each other inside me. My back arched toward her, but I wrapped my hands around my cock in defense. She tickled my sides, laughed at my squirming, and then assumed a mock serious face.

'So, are you able to take care of that... situation yourself, Mister?'

She nodded to my cock.

'Yes.'

'How do you normally do it?'

I grinned.

'I use your hand cream.'

She snatched my pillow from under my head and hit me with it.

'I knew it! I knew there was a reason why I sometimes can't find my cream! You're the thief!'

We laughed. I snatched my pillow back and shoved it under my head. She stood up from my bed, took a moment to steady herself, smoothed out the luxurious silk of her chemise, and left the room without explanation. I looked out the window and saw the cold moonlight had not abated and neither had the heat from my call with Dolly.

Mei Mei returned.

'Hey, thief. Here's a brand-new tin of the good stuff. Now you don't have to steal mine.'

She tossed me a tin of *White Peony* moisturizing cream and fell into my bed beside me. I made room on my left side for her. She grabbed herself a share of my pillow to lay her head upon.

'Thanks, Ma. A whole tin! That should last me a week, at least.'

'Don't thank me, smart ass—show me.'

'What?'

She turned her head toward me. Her eyes were half-hidden behind her mussed-up waves of thick black hair piled around her porcelain face.

'Show me how you do it.'

'Now?'

'I know you're going to do it tonight anyway. You may as well right now. Let's see if you know what you're doing.'

I sat up in my bed. She turned her body toward me. I flung aside my bed sheet like a magician revealing a hidden rabbit.

'Ta da!'

She giggled and twined her legs into mine. I imagined the way snakes make love. I opened the tin of cream, scooped up a dollop in my right hand and slathered it along my cock. She watched me and I watched her.

'I'm so happy you're regularly moisturizing *bǎo bèi*. It's important to keep your skin soft and supple.'

She laughed so hard that she rocked my bed. I smiled despite myself.

'Shut up, you. I'm concentrating.'

'So sorry,' she huffed, dripping with sarcasm.

She pressed her breasts into the side of my body and rested her hand on my shoulder. I felt her breath lap in soft waves against my neck. I conjured Dolly's voice.

Sweet dreams, qīnài de.

I hugged my cock against my body and rolled it from side to side across my tummy. It shone with moisture in the moonlight. I spread my fingers, pressed my whole length hard against my skin, and used my thumb to rub small quick circles over my fleshy head. I wondered if Dolly would like it. My breath deepened and fell in time with my stepmother's breathing.

'I'm impressed so far. You've been doing this for a while, huh?'

I grinned.

'I found your dirty books.'

She gasped in mock outrage and bit my ear.

'*Tǎo yàn*! (Disgusting naughty boy).'

Unfazed, I continued to rub and tease my head. My body tensed as if shocked by electricity with every flick of my thumb. My eyes rolled back in my head. I felt the switch in my brain that turned off all my good manners.

'My favorite story in your books is the affair between the teacher and the student.'

'She teaches him bad things.'

'Yes.'

I wanted Dolly to teach me bad things.

Mei Mei uttered a soft moan.

'Squeeze it in your fist and stroke it up and down in a corkscrew motion.'

I did as I was told. The strokes were slow and languid. I was sure she would like it like that. She rubbed her feet against mine.

'Good job. Now... may I?'

She reached out her left hand toward my cock.

'Yes, please.'

She pressed the flat of her hand over the head of my cock and drew slow circles in time with my corkscrew strokes up and down my shaft. I was spoiled with arousal from two different directions. Another soft moan fell from her mouth.

'Now you try it.'

She withdrew her hand and placed it onto my pelvis which was rocking back and forth like a ship on a stormy ocean. I pressed my left palm on top of my cock and rubbed in circles like she taught me. It took some coordination to do this whilst stroking with the other hand, but I eventually found my rhythm. I crossed my ankles and squeezed my balls between my thighs, tensing every muscle in my body. After that night, pleasuring myself would never be the same again.

'Teach me more.'

'Give me your balls.'

I unlocked my ankles, and she expertly scooped up my tight package into her left hand and yanked it downward. Everything got sharper.

'How does that feel?'

'It feels like my skin is stretched tight as a drum around my...'

'*Jūju*.'

'Yes, and it feels more... intense.'

'And how about when I do this?'

She took her hand off my balls for a moment to dip her middle finger into the tin of cream. When she resumed shoving my balls downward, she used her moisturized middle finger to search for a particularly sensitive place down below. If I were not so mad with pleasure, I would be horrified by the feeling of someone's finger gliding around the rim of my asshole. However, in that moment, she nurtured me to a place where I was comfortable tasting an entirely new flavor of arousal.

'I like that a lot. Thank you.'

'You got no choice but to like it, boy. I got you by the balls.'

I laughed out loud and kissed her on the forehead. I scooped up another dollop of moisturizer and stroked my cock harder. At the end of each corkscrew motion, I flicked my thumb over the head of my cock. She leaned into my ear and whispered.

'Now you try it.'

I did as I was told. I grabbed my own balls and fingered my own ass. I shifted up a gear to build towards an orgasm. I imagined all my pencil strokes in all my drawings of Dolly coming to life. I imagined her peeling away her clothes and any other barriers in our way. I imagined everything in the room getting sucked into the vortex of my pleasure. I remembered how nice my name sounded rolling off the end of her tongue. My biceps flexed so hard that large veins popped along their length as my hands whipped up an orgasm. When I climaxed, I could not decide if it was an explosion or an implosion. Is this what sex will feel like? Was it as good as this? Was it even better?

Meanwhile, Mei Mei was furiously playing with herself beside me. Her right hand was jammed between her thighs while her left was reaching around to the crack of her bum. Her body twisted into a spasm. She bit the fleshy part of my left bicep as she enjoyed her own orgasm. I did not feel the pain of her bite, nor did I notice the mark she made until afterward. I had not even registered that she left the room until she returned with a small hot wet towel fragranced with lavender oil. She sat on my bed beside me and pressed the folded towel gently against my forehead, my cheeks and my chest. Then she opened the towel and used it to thoroughly soak up all my cum. I made such a mess all over myself. We shared a smile. She tucked me in, kissed me goodnight on my mouth, and tottered back to her bedroom.

The next morning, I was enjoying a cup of ginseng tea by the big living room window that refused to open. I was watching, but not watching, the old ladies practicing tai chi down below in our courtyard. My father's wife woke up after me. The sharp scent of her first *Double Happiness* brand cigarette was followed by the soft scuffle of her fluffy slippers on the linoleum floor.

'Good morning, Ma.'

'Good morning! Did you and *bǎo bèi* sleep well?'

I grinned.

'Eventually.'

'I'm happy.'

She wrapped her arms around me from behind. Her body pressed into mine, separated only by her mulberry-silk chemise.

My birthday falls in the dead of Chengdu winter. On the day I turned 17, a courier wearing a thick army-surplus parka and mittens trundled a heavy box up the elevator and delivered it to our front door. I cut it open. An avalanche of foam packing beans spilled out and revealed a gargantuan Mitsubishi *CK-3501R* television.

In 1987, an entire neighborhood might share one TV. The average Chinese TV screen measured twelve inches. Our new TV was thirty-five inches. It boasted four speakers so the whole building could hear we owned something worth stealing. My father bought two of these monstrosities, one for me and one for himself.

A month prior, Mei Mei sent him a magazine clipping of filmmaker Martin Scorsese promoting the set. She remembered he enjoyed the films of Scorsese. These two grown-ups understood each other in ways I would never comprehend. I was envious. I imagined the frisson the couple may have enjoyed during their days of wine and roses. My life with my father had been interrupted. He was clumsily filling this void by sending me wondrous inanimate things.

Mei Mei agreed to let me have a modest birthday party with Dolly, Lily, and Cici on the condition that she chaperone.

'Why all three friends have to be women?' she asked with a pinched look I could not quite interpret.

Any answer I may have given would have added fuel to her fire of discontent. Her high-toned voice reaching new heights.

'Why invite nobody from your school? Ask some kids your age. Those women are not normal friends of a schoolboy like you! It's not healthy like this.'

Was she right? Should I be more normal? There were consequences for people who were not normal in our little big world of China.

For the first time, I scanned our apartment and imagined the first impression our home made upon our visitors. It was demonstrably clear Mei Mei loved pastels. All of our conspicuously modern furnishings, appliances, and knick-knacks were chosen less for their function and more for their color: cool blue, mint green, pale peach, rose blush, blanched lavender, and of course, coral pink. She designed a home to be both endearing in its colorful charm and intimidating in its deliberate affect.

Mei Mei unsealed her 1972 Halston dress for my birthday party. She had my father organize an associate in New York to bid on the Halston at a deceased estate auction. She took every opportunity to boast it was the same pale flaxen dress the designer made for actress Angelica Huston. Actually, it was only ever worn by a dead socialite. The Halston was cut on the bias so that it skimmed her body as she moved. When she wore the dress, she exuded the throwaway chic of a playful nymph attending an ancient Roman court or perhaps a Gatsby soirée. She seemed compelled to peacock her wardrobe for my guests.

They arrived shortly after nightfall. Lily and Cici were the first to spill across our doorway. They looked like Madonna and Cindi Lauper had mixed up the contents of their respective wardrobes. I was so happy they came, and we enjoyed a group hug. Mei Mei, however, looked like she was trying to smile while sucking on a lemon.

Then Dolly entered. She wore Western clothes I never saw her wear before that night. I found her new look disarming because I was used to her myriad of qipao dresses. I lost my voice and took the longest moment to respond.

'Hi... I am glad you came.'

'I wouldn't miss it. You only turn 17 once. You're growing up so fast before my very eyes.'

She leaned in and brushed my cheek with a kiss that was meant to be chaste, but it made me feel otherwise. Her heady scent and warm breath was left behind like an imprint on my skin. I became seriously aware of my stepmother in the room while my head was swimming in the narcotic presence of Dolly.

Her glorious hair was styled into a voluminous halo. She wore a sharp black blazer with a teasing reveal of red satin lining. Under the blazer, she wore a white silk top. The strong matt finish of her blazer complimented the sheen of her pants that hugged her coltish legs like second skin. Her ankle boots, geometric earrings, and envelope clutch purse were all a shade of red that rang sirens in my head. To match her blouse, a long snow-white coat was folded over her arm. I was picturing how svelte she would have looked walking into our courtyard wearing this wide-lapel garment cinched tight at her narrow waist. I bet there was a pair of matching fire-engine-red gloves in the pocket of her soft woolen coat. The dramatic black, red, and white palette she fashioned was signaling something I wanted to decode. I snapped out of my stupor enough to make introductions between the two most important women in my life.

'Dolly, this is my stepmother, Mei Mei.'

The two women greeted one another with smiles that did not quite reach their eyes.

Mei Mei graciously collected coats from all three ladies and draped them over her armchair. She then laid out plates of sliced oranges, watermelon, and best of all, her extra flaky scallion pancakes. They were Mei Mei's specialty hors d'oeuvres. These golden triangles were made from layer upon crispy layer of pastry flavored with the tangy zest of seasoned scallions. The carefully crafted layering was the secret reason why her pancakes were so loved by her family.

Lily and Cici swooned over the size of our new television. I switched it on from across the room using the big forty-one button remote control. The reaction from the girls was the same as if I conjured a magic trick. They had never seen *CCTV* (State television) displayed so excessively large before.

I showed them how to search through stations using the infra-red remote control. The girls flipped channels looking for the popular series, *Journey to the West*. They had lots of questions about the National *NV-300* video cassette recorder I wired up to the television. Never had they seen a home-video system before.

I watched Mei Mei watch Dolly with shrewd interest. Dolly was the voguish and sophisticated woman of the eighties. Whereas Mei Mei was the elegant waif of the seventies. My stepmother cast a glance at me and then back to Dolly and then to me again. She was telegraphing a signal that was outside my frequency range. She wore an expression of protective concern blended with something else more potent known only to her. There were occasions when my stepmother was an unfathomable mystery to me. Sometimes the human heart is too slippery to hold in your hand for more than a brief moment.

DOLLY

I never wanted to be predictable. To this end I planned to show a different side of me for David's birthday party. I told myself I'd dress in something different for some light fun. However, as I invested more and more time into this idea, it grew into a project that exposed how much I wanted to impress him.

I altered a boy's blazer to suit my figure. I restyled a silk blouse to mimic a piece worn by Gia Carangi. The pants were cut from a pattern I drafted by disassembling some old pants I was throwing out anyway. The coat was a gift from a Canadian customer. The boots and clutch took a while to source because they *had* to match my blazer's red lining. My earrings were made from some plastic component pieces I found. I painted them with my siren red nail color to match the other red elements. I then glued small plain flat earrings to them with epoxy resin. The look was sealed with my *Shiseido* red lips.

I reached out to one of my customers who owned the *Lucky Girl* hair salons. I always said hello to his wife at the markets. He generously booked me a free full-service appointment at his closest salon. I felt this was only fair seeing as how many times I gave him the full-service.

I looked great but I should have worn gloves. I was freezing. We ran through David's courtyard to get inside, out of the cold. I stumbled in the fresh snow. The girls helped me to my feet and brushed the snowflakes from my coat. I'm glad I fell. I needed a moment to take a breath. The air was thick with the fragrance of Wintersweet flowers. My heart slowed to a reasonable pace. We entered his foyer.

I was happy David chose something to wear that would knock a girl's socks off. He looked grown-up in a deep jade collared shirt that made his green eyes pop. His pressed and perfectly fitted black trousers were a welcome change from the jeans he always wore. Those *Levi's* didn't hug his ass like they should. He was totally handsome. That's all I'll say about that.

From the instant she set her eyes upon me, I felt his stepmother recognised something in me. It was as if she'd marked me. She was friendly, but not friendly,

'Pleased to meet you... Dolly, is it? That's an unusual Western name.'

'It's an American singer that I like...'

'Oh, I can't listen to that foreign music. Only Mandopop for me. Funny that David never mentioned you, no?'

I refused to be rattled and instead, showed some cheek.

'Well, I must be his little secret, yes?'

She and I shared polite laughter only bitches share. Mei Mei stepped closer to me.

'I see that you're the same age as me.'

She pointed to the little jade dog dangling from my bracelet.

'You and I were born in the Year of the Dog—1958. I used to have a trinket just like it. Threw it away. Bit old fashioned now.'

My little jade friend was a hasty last-minute addition to my outfit. I never wore him at work. Mei Mei was on a roll with the age issue.

'David is also Year of the Dog, but he was born in 1970, you understand? Much, much younger.'

We shared that bitchy laugh again while the other two girls in the room seemed perplexed as if we were speaking an unfamiliar dialect.

I felt Mei Mei was determined to draw a triangle of tension between herself, David, and me. Nevertheless, I saw no disgust from David at the mention of my age. There was nothing but the same open face he always gave me. He seemed oblivious to the under-words spoken by his stepmother.

I spent the rest of the night observing my new acquaintance and her stepson. She was far too handsy with him. It gave me a prickly feeling. She was always touching him in places close to "girlfriend-only areas" of his body. His response to her touches held clues I was beginning to solve. I was sure she lacked the skill to touch him in the way I could. Did his stepmother understand what us girls do for a living? Did Mei Mei suspect something about David and me? Surely not. Surely no one would suspect a boy like David would want an old woman like me. I shouldn't care, for fucks' sake!

Anyway, we enjoyed a bootleg copy of the movie *The Day That Ferris Bueller Has Off* with Mandarin dubs.

DAVID

A mountain of dumplings was my preferred terrible food choice for late night cravings. The best stress-dumplings in my neighborhood were sold by a couple I came to know well—Andy and Coco. They served delicious meals from a hole-in-the-wall only one block from my home. I paid the couple in paper money, and never waited for change. Andy fried up a mess of pork dumplings flavored with chopped chives and ground Szechuan peppercorns. Meanwhile, Coco would fill a dipping bowl with rich garlic sauce mixed with Szechuan chillies, finely chopped fresh shallots, and a dash of Chinkiang vinegar. This last vital ingredient infused the mix with a unique malty, woody, smoked flavor. The taste of Coco's special sauce soothed my palate for hours afterwards.

I carried my warm carton of treasures to the shop's seating area—one folding table on the sidewalk and two folding chairs. Sometimes, there was only one chair as the nearby mah-jong players would borrow its sibling. They gathered their playing pieces in their eager hands only to lay them out like runes promising only good fortune.

The sharp clacking of the mah-jong tiles was oddly comforting. So were the random sizzling of insects getting fried to death in the big bug zapper hung near the mah-jong crew. Every bite of the oily crunchy spicy dumplings eased my hungry disposition, at least temporarily.

I was thinking of the small imperfections we love in another while they are trying their best to be perfect. I adored the way Dolly said the names of Western films the wrong way round. She told me she thought the boy from *The Kid Who Makes Karate* was cute. Whenever she was struggling to explain a song she heard or a novel she read, she would give up on words and let her lovely complex hand gestures speak. She created shapes in the air more sophisticated than mere speech. Dolly looked so good on my birthday. It was as if I had discovered her all over again.

What was my next move? If I was the author of my own story, how would I develop the shape of its arc? Was she writing this plot with me?

The bug zapper flared bright blue as a big moth was burnt to a crisp. I squashed up my empty carton and dirty napkins and dumped them in a bin outside *Gao's Shoe Repairs.* I waved goodnight to Andy and Coco. Too wound up to go home just yet, I took the long way back. I wondered if my dumpling binge was feeding only one of my two cravings.

The business quarter was lit with the most sodium-vapor streetlamps in my neighborhood. Nightfall will transform a street into a dark stage suggesting an abyss outside the pools of yellow light. Although the hour was late, there was a small ensemble of people with roles to play. I was less lonely in their company.

An elderly lady in a puffy vest-jacket swept dirt from the sidewalk onto the street. She waved to a man peddling an empty samlor carriage. A black cat dashed out of his way. Black cats are a sign of good luck in China.

From somewhere above I heard a woman's voice. Her coquettish words were dipped in sleaze.

'Hello, young man.'

Very few windows were lit above the shops. One particular window was filled with the glow of red fluorescent light and a face to match the voice. Her broad smile held teeth that seemed too big.

'Are you looking for someone?'

'No. Yes. Maybe.'

'No, yes, and maybe.'

'I don't know.'

'You do not know.'

Her answers were statements, not questions. She was a perfect echo. People began staring at me talking to the red-light lady. She must have noticed as well.

'Meet me downstairs. There is a door. I will open it for you.'

I was not even thinking. I was simply moving. Certain women's voices took over the reins of my body.

1352 was stenciled above her door. It was papered over with pages from Shanghai gossip magazines. They were torn away in places to reveal paint the color of an old blood stain. The door cracked open to reveal the face I saw in the window.

Up close, I could discern the thick black strokes of kohl eyeliner she had drawn around her eyes. Her artistic flourishes would be the envy of Nefertiti. However, her beauty spot was real, not drawn, just like Madonna. The mark lay above the right side of her mouth and drew your eye to her lined lips. Her teeth were hidden behind a Mona Lisa smile. She wore a red dress split so high at the sides, it was in danger of splitting in half at any moment.

'I am Liling.'

Her name was literally the sound of white jasmine.

'My name's... John.'

'Come inside... John.'

I did as I was told. We locked eyes as she reached around me to close the door. I tasted the whiskey on her breath and felt the first threads of a web being spun between us. She motioned for me to follow her upstairs. Again, I was simply moving. With every step she took, her dress flashed a river of alabaster skin running from her legs, sweeping over her bum, and up to her waist. She was white flesh wrapped in a red flame, a promise to light a fire in the dark.

The staircase ended with one room. It was bathed in the red light I saw from the street. On the windowsill, a cigarette rested precariously on the lip of an ashtray. Tendrils of smoke rose like charmed snakes. A shower recess in the corner was shrouded with a plastic curtain printed with blue lotus flowers. She sat on the edge of a queen-sized bed and smoothed her hand over its linen printed with more blue lotus.

'Sit with me.'

I did as I was told.

'You are a virgin, John.'

Our eyes locked once more.

'I'm a virgin.'

'You would prefer not to be.'

'Yes.'

'How much am I worth to you?'

Her expression was smooth. She was the calm surface of a lake at dawn before the winds broke the tension. I counted in my head how many bills were in my pocket.

Folded white towels were stacked on a chipped veneer dresser. A plastic laundry basket was filled with used towels and some underwear. The hem of her dress was frayed in places. I fought an urge to pull at her loose threads. This was a garment she must have worn within an inch of its life. Her hair was matted at the back where she could not see it in a mirror. Her foundation needed repainting as much as the walls. Her imperfections revealed a person underneath with whom I wanted to talk more than anything else she had to offer. The web spinning between us melted away and was replaced with something stronger. She must have registered my sober appraisal.

'You have a question.'

A panel of mirrored glass was stuck to the wall near the doorway.

'Liling, do you ever know who you are?'

A small tension pulled at the corner of her left eye.

'No, not all. Pieces of me spin off as I move from one man to another. I travel without a permit nor passport from one body to the next. Sometimes the transition is not as smooth as it should be.'

She smiled so swiftly that I was unsure if I had seen a smile at all. I caught a flash of Dolly in her eyes. How could two women share such similar life choices and yet live those lives so differently?

An upside-down crate served as a bedside table. On top of the crate, there was a boar-bristle hairbrush, a digital alarm clock, and a plastic squirt-bottle of baby oil. I picked up the brush, crossed my legs behind her, and gently pulled the bristles through her hair. Did my new friend bear the same burdens as Dolly?

'Do you ever tire of the trickery?'

'Tricks are not what I sell. Everyone thinks that. I deal in absolution. Men come to me wanting a confessor. There are things they cannot share with their own people.'

I brushed out the tangles from her hair until it was smooth again. I combed her tresses away from her face with my fingers. Hidden underneath her hair, on the nape of her neck, was a red and green tattoo.

我是我的
(I am mine).

The red calligraphy was underlined by a sleek green dragon. If women were tattooed in those days, it was typically a brand enforced upon a woman's skin by a possessive pimp. Only the most renegade women bore ink of their own design. I wondered how she earned this mark? I wondered what was left for her to claim?

'You deserve your own absolution.'

'Perhaps. I want my mother to forgive me. She was an academic, a published scholar. She taught me all the classic literature, both East and West. One day I was told by The Party to stop reading and work in the factories. We made tractors.'

'Where's your mother now?'

'She is dead.'

'She died. You found a way out of the factory. Most of all, you want to forgive yourself.'

'Why is it so easy to tell you these things?'

We jumped at the sound of a commotion outside and dashed to the window. As soon as she saw it was the police, she switched off her red light. We were now two scared children witnessing four policemen drag a man and woman into the street. This was not the self-righteous thuggery of overzealous police. This was something far more awful. They were professional bullies. One of them took a swig of liquor from a bottle. He passed it to his comrade so he could bludgeon the man with his baton. He cried out with each beating. He fell silent when he was struck hard across the skull. His body collapsed. A dark pool spread on the street around his prone body. The woman unleashed a scream like a siren of raw grief. A policeman smacked her so hard across her face that I felt it from the upper floor as if it were a thunderclap.

'Shut up, whore!'

She was silent but shaking with fear and anger. I could see her convulsions from across the distance between us. Her dress had ridden up above her waist, and she was trying to pull it down. A raised baton stopped her from moving at all. My companion fell into a lunatic calm beside me.

'It is the end of the world, young man. Go home. There is a back way. I will show you.'

She guided me to a window on the opposite end of the room. A ledge outside joined with a rooftop. It led to a back street. As I climbed through the window, I held out my hand to her. She took it, and the folded cash in my palm. We locked eyes one final time and disappeared from each other's lives.

I took so many wrong turns in my panic to find home. Once I was on the safe side of my locked and bolted door, I made a cup of chamomile tea to slow my racing heart. I gazed out at the courtyard from my chair at the big living room window that refused to open. I half-expected the policemen to appear there. I imagined them following me like monsters in a horror film who do not give up until everyone is dead. In the silence, I recognised how absurdly protected I was because of what I am and to whom I am connected. The horror show kept replaying over and over behind my retinas where the memory was forever burnt. The woman's cry rang in my ears just as it had ricocheted between the buildings like a wounded and frightened banshee.

That poor couple could have been Andy and Coco. It could have been my friends down there getting violated and butchered.

The bullies were getting worse, and I had not even noticed the escalation of terror while I sat in my comfy apartment and sipped my fucking chamomile.

DOLLY

A sunny day in Chengdu was a rare joy. Our ashen sky seldom turned a rich clear blue. The naked sun was greeted like a long lost friend, except for the dogs that barked in surprise at the bright yellow intruder in the strange blue sky.

Such a day galvanized the Szechuanese soul. Many of us would take the day off to relax at an outdoor teahouse. My personal favorite was the century-old *Singing Crane* in People's Park. I enjoyed the view of the lake from where I sat on one of the scattered chairs fashioned from bamboo and wicker. Children threw clumsy fistfuls of fish food at the golden koi teeming under the lake's surface. A big fat frog croaked from deep under the decking. There was a sharp click of mah-jong tiles from a small group behind me. From other tables, the slap of playing cards. I heard before I saw the ear cleaner. He touted his services by striking musical notes from his metal tongs. I still hear the sounds of the teahouse in my dreams.

Teahouses have been around since the Tang Dynasty. By the end of the nineteenth century, there was one on every street in Chengdu. A teahouse is a lot more than somewhere to go for tea. Traders would do business from them, legal or otherwise. Most importantly, a teahouse served as a social switchboard for the latest news and gossip.

The tea leaves were served in a sachet with a cup with a lid and a large flask of boiled water. I was the only customer strange enough to wash my leaves before I drank from them. I poured the boiled water over the leaves, placed the lid on top of the cup, leaving the slightest gap, and tipped my cup beside my chair, allowing the water to drain out into the lake. Now the leaves were clean enough for me to steep them in more boiled water and drink from them.

There's an art to drinking tea. Some people grasp the saucer with one hand, lift the lid with the other and use it to scoop away floating leaves. I preferred to hold the cup by the rim with my thumb and middle finger. I used my index finger to push aside the lid only far enough to let the tea flow while filtering out the leaves.

I enjoyed the company of an old deaf lady named Jing at *Singing Crane*. She knitted endless scarves while I told her all my secrets. I'd spill all sorts of awful things she couldn't possibly hear. Guilt is a burden we can't bear alone.

In between my confessions, I munched on roasted sunflower seeds like a mad woman. I always bought a big bag of the garlic variety at the market on the way to *Singing Crane*. Similar to tea, there was an art to eating sunflower seeds. You have to wedge the pointed end of the seed sideways between your front teeth and crack the husk twice. I used the tip of my tongue to discern the soft kernel from the sharp split husk, teased the prize into my mouth and devoured it. There's an equal degree of art to telling secrets. The trick was to make sure your secrets are never heard.

As I spilled my guilt to my deaf friend, my pile of empty husks on the table grew larger by the minute.

'It all began as a fun distraction to let David hang out with us crazy girls. We sing, eat, and joke around. However, something unexpected has found safe harbor deep inside me. It was getting harder to hide it. It outgrows my self-control. The more I feel this way, the more I want to shout it from the rooftop. Instead, I scream it into my pillow so the neighbors won't hear.'

I felt as much satisfaction purging these things as I did when cracking the seeds between my teeth. Jing nodded silently. She looked up from her knitting at intervals and smiled at me.

'I'm afraid of people's reaction to my pursuing this boy. Then again, I'm not afraid. I've always enjoyed a dare. I'm more afraid of how much I want him. Until now, I've felt comfortable having the two other girls in the space between him and I. Lily and Cici form a buffer zone. Secretly, I sometimes want him to myself. How do I get him alone?'

I stopped spilling for a moment when something caught my eye. A pair of kites flying clear of the tall trees. The March winds whipped up the air around the pair. One kite was a psychedelic butterfly. The other, a bird made of all the colors of the rainbow. They caught and held the high winds as if they were never coming down. It may take all of my courage to feel safe enough to fly so high and trust the wind.

DAVID

Dolly surprised me with a telephone call one Thursday night. She wanted me to rendezvous with her at a karaoke competition after school the following evening. We never sang in front of a crowd. Why did she want to sing in public all of a sudden? Why did she choose a night outside of our routine? Why were Lily and Cici not included? This felt important like it was a school assignment.

Dolly asked me to learn a duet that had been charting all over the world. I found a bootleg copy of a copy of a copy of the song and popped it into my *Walkman*. All day Friday, I practiced the words whilst drawing in art class with my headphones snapped on. I was sure every student and teacher found me quite peculiar. I mouthed the words of the popular duet while the music filled my ears.

After the school bell rang, I dashed out to the bicycle rack only to find my bike was stolen. Bicycle theft was so prevalent in China that I was not even surprised. I would run to her instead.

I sprinted through the backstreet labyrinth of Chengdu, dodging Dan-Dan soup sellers, side-stepping samlor drivers, and flying through alleys no larger than crawlspaces. I tore a hole in my school blazer and threw it away. I was gasping for air, so I unknotted my school tie and tossed it away.

Finally, the *Shangri-La Karaoke Bar* was in my sight, a mere block away. I was late!

DOLLY

I'd waited alone on stage long enough for David. I was sad he stood me up. I was looking forward to sharing the atmosphere with him. He enjoyed this kind of scene. *The Shangri-La* was straight out of a film noir. The actual bar was rich dark mahogany from a British pub whose owners fled the country the year Mao "liberated" China. In fact, everything in the place was salvaged from Western nightclubs shut down decades ago. The well-worn stools, warm leatherette booths, and frosty beer taps were all nostalgic relics of a golden age before communism. When I discovered the *Shangri-La*, my first thought was David would love it.

I felt like I was a bridegroom abandoned at the altar. I worried the audience would feel my loneliness, so I pretended I didn't care. After all, this was a guise I was accustomed to wearing.

The music began and I moved my feet side-to-side in time with the opening bars of my song. This track was fresh and trendy enough so the audience recognised it from the opening bars. A roar of approval rose from the fifty or so people at the bar. At first, there was a tease of a synth drum. This was followed by a guitar riff hook. It got my whole body moving. I found the words. Aretha Franklin is tough to copy. It was a voice from a deeper part of me than I am used to. As I sang the first verse, David burst through the doors. He rushed the stage, grabbed a microphone, and took his place beside me. I had my George Michael. The crowd stood up and cheered for this unexpected melodrama. David launched into the second verse of *I Knew You Were Waiting.*

He was beautiful. I smiled so hard. I wondered how my mouth would form the words. We shared a chorus of faith and belief that spiraled upward and out across the crowd. I held onto his arm like a fool with clouds in my eyes. He was there where I wanted him. He came through when I needed him. David was the hero I asked him to be for me. This small, dumb request of mine was met without question. This silly gesture was more than anyone else had done for me. Plus, I was singing a duet with a handsome young man in front of an audience!

We finished our song to a deafening applause from a standing crowd. I spied the karaoke judges to the right of me tallying up our scores. I squeezed his hand in mine.

DAVID

At the end of the night, I walked Dolly home while holding our little trophy. We strolled as leisurely as possible, to drag the night out before the spell was broken. She and I held close to one another for warmth against the crisp cool air. Winter was a time when you could smell rows of sausage curing in windows. These Szechuan delicacies were spiced with cumin and cardamom and preserved in orange zest and rich liqueurs. I felt hungry in more ways than one.

A flower vendor mistook us for a couple, and he offered us a bouquet of deep red carnations. We had fun playing along with the fantasy. I bought the flowers and laid them in the cradle of Dolly's arm.

We stopped at a street corner in the Wuhou District. Moths danced under the streetlamp. She showed me her favorite house. There was something daring and Dolly-esque about this sleek, linear, geometric 1920s home. It was flagrantly Western.

'This is one of the last art-deco buildings that Chairman Mao must have forgotten to tear down.'

'What was his problem with these beautiful buildings?'

'Oh, *qīnài de*. You're so sweet and innocent sometimes! Mao saw the art-deco style as an expression of Western decadence. We used to have the world's greatest collection of art-deco architecture until the day we didn't. You Westerners and your corrupting influence needed to be eradicated like a pest.'

She laughed and surprised me with a slap on my bum. Her brazen familiarity with my body and her schooling me in history sent a delicious thrill down to my toes. I was filled with an unexpected desire to allow her complete license to do whatever she wished with me. Was this what love is meant to feel like? Did I desire a kind of submission?

'See? You enter the house this way.'

She held my arm, leaned close to me, and pointed down an avenue lined with splendid Wutong trees. Their trunks pale as parchment. Their sawtooth leaves like crisp slices of green glass that filtered the moonlight.

'I sometimes imagine enjoying the view of the Fuhe River from up there. I dream of sitting on the porch, or even the lawn, sipping tea. I wonder if everything would feel like it's in the right place if...?'

She abruptly laughed at herself. 'I gotta stop dreaming, it's no good for me, for fucks' sake!'

Though we retired to our separate homes, I dreamt of waking up with her in my arms.

DOLLY

There were a dozen ways I held David in my sleep.

Four

DAVID

I was so busy with my final senior art project at school I did not visit Dolly as much as I wanted. My study partner was Jolin. The origin story of our relationship followed every absurd romance cliché.

It was far too common in our life classes for the students to choose me, the funny-looking foreigner, as the subject. This was part of a larger practice in the Chinese art world whereby foreign faces were fetishised. One day, I insisted someone else be our subject. I scanned the room and my eyes fell upon Jolin. I said to my classmates that I saw in Jolin an undeniable beauty. I challenged the room to see what I saw. So, they did. The result was spectacular. We dedicated an entire public exhibit to every painted, sketched, and pastelled portrayal of our Jolin. She walked through the gallery filled with images of herself. She was smiling and giddy with delight as if it were a hall of mirrors reflecting back her fresh, winsome charm.

Our teacher required all her art students to find a partner for our term-four assignment. Jolin sidled up to me, her face deeply flushed, and asked for my hand in academic matrimony. So began the romance-story sensation of the school year. The *gweilo* finally chose a sweetheart. Regrettably, no one bothered to consult me about it.

Mei Mei was already mapping out my courtship with Jolin. She told me how handsome I would look in a smart double-breasted suit on my wedding day. Jolin was deemed by my stepmother as the "right type", and most importantly the right age. Ever since my birthday party, Mei Mei had taken every opportunity to point out how Dolly and the girls were the "wrong type" of women. She insisted a nice boy like me should not be associated with that type.

Jealousy can reveal itself in convoluted ways. I saw fear in her eyes and heard anger in her voice whenever she spoke of Dolly. Jealousy can also be appeased in the most unexpected ways. I came to understand this whenever Jolin visited our home. There is a dance that a girl performs for her potential mother-in-law. Jolin displayed modesty and reverence toward Mei Mei. Her benign personality assured my stepmother Jolin was a manageable threat. She would not intoxicate me. She would never consume me so much that I was no longer Mei's boy.

My stepmother often lectured me about the best and worst women as I was rubbing her feet after Sunday Markets. She would sit up in her bed after a shower, rest her feet on my lap, and have me massage a particular place in her sole. She told me this pressure point was connected to her heart. I doubt she was in any real pain. I believed she simply enjoyed someone taking care of her and listening.

'Remember that tall widow lady who lived on the top floor?'

'Yes, Ma.'

'...and Mrs Xui's nice son who lived on the bottom?'

'Yes, Ma.'

'They got caught together and now their families never talk to them. See what happens?'

'Oh wow. I didn't know that. How terrible.'

I lied. I had been following their tender romance from the beginning. My journals contained sketches of their dalliances in the stairwell, and their midnight liaisons down in the courtyard playground. The subtle shades of light and dark enjoyed by the fated couple was not something I felt with Jolin. She and I were nothing more than the faint outline of a love story.

On the surface, our narrative seemed to be adhering to the standard three-act structure of a romance novel. Jolin and I had progressed to the first plot point. This is when the two lead characters find themselves in a situation where they are stuck with each other, for example, building an art installation for our final grade.

There were many weekends I had to let Dolly know I could not karaoke with the girls. I told her I wanted to spend Saturday evenings workshopping with Jolin. Both Lily and Cici were crestfallen, but Dolly seemed unperturbed. She wished me luck in my studies while she filed her index nail.

Jolin and I enjoyed long, lively discussions at either her place or mine. We talked about anything and everything late into the night. She loved to outwit me with her acumen for art and history. I was happy to bathe in the fountain of her knowledge. It became difficult to focus on the task at hand—we needed to create a piece indicative of the New Wave of Chinese Art.

She also baked cookies. When I visited her home for the first time, she pulled from the oven a hot tray of coconut macarons. The rich smell of these sweet lumps of shredded coconut with a golden crust made my eyes roll back in delight. I relished the perfectly balanced hard and soft parts of her cookies. She was an artist in more ways than one.

She liked to tell the stories behind everything.

'This recipe came from the French court of Henry the Second. They were baked by chefs the king's wife brought from Italy. I always feel like this sixteenth-century cookie needs a little something extra from the twentieth-century. So, I like to serve them with...'

She pulled two greenglass bottles of *Coca-Cola* from her fridge and expertly snapped off the tops with a bread knife. I grinned at her. She was one of the coolest girls I knew, and simultaneously, a bigger dork than me.

I met her parents in their tastefully understated living room. All three of them reminded me of those perfectly cast family units you saw on CCTV commercials for soap or rice cookers. They all shared the same good skin and easy smiles. I envied the ordinary family bond they shared. I wished I knew what it was like to live a life that was blissfully unsurprising.

She and I enjoyed a camaraderie I would never find in another person. We shared a feeling something was happening in Chinese art no one was expecting, least of all the establishment.

Jolin brought some of her most treasured books to school to show me. Her collection was incredible. Most were books on art, some were first editions, and all of them were worn out from reading. I felt honored she let me borrow her hardcover copy of Thomas Wolfe's 1975 critique, *The Painted Word*. We discussed it in class when I returned her book as promised. We were sitting in our favorite chairs by the giant industrial window.

'David, I told you that you'd eat it up.'

'The best part was when Wolfe says, *Aesthetics is for the artists as ornithology is for the birds*.'

'Yes! It's not just another critique of art, it is a critique of critics. The gatekeepers are hurting our craft, right?'

'I always felt like critics, dealers, and even the government have a lot to answer for.'

She leaned in close to me and whispered conspiratorially.

'Better not talk about the government. You know what happens when we talk about those guys.' She touched my shoulder and grinned. Was she looking for a reason to enjoy the intimacy of a secret with me?

I studied the frames she had built for our piece. She was a big fan of the impresario frame-artist, Yasuo Minegawa. In the not-too-distant future, her work would surpass Minegawa.

She showed me her detailed plans for our installation. She was gifted with the steadiest, most precise drawing hand I have ever known. I looked at her and smiled approvingly. Her pupils dilated to the size of quail eggs. Though she wore no makeup, her cheeks appeared permanently rouged with blush.

I was not blind. I knew why she was so animated around me. I was choosing to ignore it. I drew a fine gossamer curtain between myself and whatever was simmering underneath her gaze.

One rainy day we shared my blue umbrella on our way to my apartment. She slipped whilst stepping over a puddle. She let out a yelp. I braced her against me to keep her from falling. Her stumble may or may not have been an accident. We arrived at my street corner and waited for a gap in the traffic so we could cross. She huddled closer under the shelter of my umbrella. I fought the urge to laugh out loud at the rather stubborn romance narrative stalking us.

I gleaned much of what I had learned about kissing from the film, *Endless Love*. Mei Mei and I enjoyed the film many times together. We always shared a big bowl of dragon's eye berries while calling out our favorite lines.

Mine: "I think that night, that night that I came down and saw you with Jade and then made love to my husband… I was making love to you."

Hers: "Just because you're fucking my sister doesn't make you part of the family."

Mei Mei told me she fantasized about kissing Martin Hewitt. I confided I imagined kissing Brooke Shields.

'What would my first kiss feel like?'

'My beautiful boy, you need to practice on someone before the real thing.'

On the street corner, the traffic was relentless. Jolin and I were going to be waiting awhile. I caught her gaze and she looked away. Her blush was deep. The rain fell on my blue umbrella, the traffic hummed. I kept looking at her profile, inviting her to return my soft gaze. By slow and careful increments, she looked up into my eyes again. A raindrop ran down the length of her jawbone.

I should not have, but I did it. I was only practicing. I was only thinking of myself. I was not thinking about the person who was about to return my kiss. She was not practicing.

I lowered my umbrella so we were cocooned in privacy. I leaned in for the same kiss I saw a dozen times in *Endless Love*. She made it too easy. Our lips locked like warm soft puzzle pieces. She welcomed me as if she were dying of thirst and she hoped my lips were water. With my free hand, I reached out and touched her small chin. I slowly traced my fingertip along the wet line of her jaw until I reached her soft earlobe. I held her bottom lip in my mouth for a beat, just like Martin had done to Brooke. Jolin let out a small sigh. I could feel her body shiver even though it was not a cold rain. Chengdu weather was always hot and sticky when wet. She lowered the umbrella further. I could feel her wanting to collapse us both into the small world she dreamt for us.

The traffic eased, but the rain did not. We decided to dash across the road, weaving between buses and rickshaw drivers to the other side. We hurried through my courtyard, and finally made it to the shelter of the foyer. As we waited for the lift. She surprised me by slipping her hands around my waist and hooking her thumbs into my belt. This time it was she who gazed softly into my eyes waiting for mine to lock with hers. I relented and met her gaze. I saw a thirst in her eyes that was not quenched. In my head, I heard the aria from *Madama Butterfly*.

Tienti la tua paura
Io con sicura fede
L'aspetto
(I with secure faith wait for him).

Would she wait for me, just as I waited in vain for my father? I felt nothing except the treachery of an actor who has fooled his audience. I saw none of the lovely shades of light and dark I witnessed in the doomed couple on our stairwell. I drew the fine gossamer curtain back into place between Jolin and I.

DOLLY

I despised myself.

For the last month, I'd been skipping lunch to spy on David and this Jolin girl through a window at their school. I went through his daily planner one day and found out they always attended the same class at 12.30 Tuesdays and Thursdays. Lucky for me, he kept such a ridiculously detailed schedule, and copious diary notes—which were a guilty pleasure to devour. I figured out which room was theirs by asking a teacher who was also my customer. There was a bus stop bench opposite the classroom. From this vantage point, I had an eyeline to a floor-to-ceiling window where they always sat together. I pretended to be waiting for a bus while I smoked cigarettes and chewed my nails. I kept staring at them until I ached. She seemed... nice. That's all I'll say about that. The hunger I felt from skipping lunches was nothing compared to the other unnameable way I felt famished. I had to cut the bullshit, for fucks' sake! He was better off pairing up with someone his own age.

Nevertheless, I watched. She mirrored him. She walked in step with his steps. She was forever leaning toward him, lightly touching his shoulder for no fucking reason. That girl looked into his eyes more than most people can bear. She played with her hair. She played with her hands. She fidgeted. Sometimes my heart would ache for her because I shared the same delicious burning itch. I bet the poor girl didn't know I was a character in this drama. I doubted she knew there were actually three of us dancing in this crisis ballet.

I was left squirming in a mess of my own making. The fight to quit my creepy habit was equally as frustrating as the struggle to articulate how I felt toward him. I felt awkward whenever I tried to say something to him. I fumbled with words. I substituted speech for ridiculous hand gestures. The memory of my hands flailing wildly in front of him while my feelings remain unexpressed made me cringe at least twice a day. He must think I'm the biggest dork. No wonder he found another girl. I bet her bedroom is not messy like mine. She looked totally neat and tidy. Isn't that what he needed? Wild messy girls like me were only useful to guys for a test drive. After they've had their fun, guys will leave a girl like me. They move on to invest in a more sensible, reliable model. Fuck that. Why should a woman be limited to play only one of only two roles?! I hate that our stories are limited, and the casting of our characters so brutally narrow.

Last night, I tore apart my home to find my pipa (a two-thousand-year-old stringed instrument). It was buried under a pile of contraband *LIFE* and *Vogue* magazines. My pipa was the closest thing to a guitar I had. I threw one leg over my window sill and strummed melancholy chords. I'd become that stupid bitch who pines for some stupid boy. I sang like a forlorn mariachi.

'He's just seventeen years-old
Leave him alone, they say
Separated by fools
Who don't know what love is yet
And I want him to know
If I could fly

I'd pick him up
I'd steal him into the night
And show him my love
That he's never seen, never seen...'

I was expecting my neighbor to bang on the wall by now. Perhaps she was a kindred spirit who understood my heartache and was letting me vent. Or maybe she wasn't home. I launched into another delightful dirge.

'Jolin, Jolin, Jolin, Jo-lin
I'm beggin' you please don't take my man
Jolin, Jolin, Jolin, Jo-lin
Please don't take him just 'cause you can
Your beauty is beyond compare
With gorgeous locks of chocolate hair
With ivory skin and the blackest eyes I've ever seen
Jolin.'

I sang my heart out until the stray dogs began howling. The old lady across the street yelled profanities at me from her window. My mewling finally ceased. I remained on my window sill for another hour staring out at the pools of street-light. One foot swinging restlessly back and forth in the empty space outside my window.

David lived a comfortable life. His *gweilo* status afforded him immunity the rest of us didn't enjoy. He never felt the cruel hand of the government take everything away. What would it be like to walk in his shoes, walk between the raindrops? I wanted him to understand what it is like to feel the full force of the storm. How would he even begin to understand I was damaged and then carefully reassembled? My spirit was blanched white. I had to paint my colors all over again. The tints and shades were never quite the same again. What remained of me was a contradiction. My parlor is immaculate. Whereas, my home looked like a mad woman's knitting. Anyone who entered my room would have to navigate around piles and piles of books revealing an obsession with Western literature. I looked around at my mess. I wondered who in their right mind would share this space with me?

I dug around and found a pack of *Lesser Panda* cigarettes. I returned to my windowsill where I continued brooding like some bitch from a Brontë book. The smoke was a bitter comfort. What I totally needed was sweetness. By that time of night, cigarettes lose their buzz and you're only smoking them out of habit. I was deciding which habit was easier to kick.

DAVID

When I showed up at her parlor one day, Dolly said she was booked out for the weekend and could not see me.

'What can I say? I'm a popular girl.'

She smirked, smacking gum in the side of her mouth.

The place was empty, save for Lily and Cici who were quiet as mice in the kitchenette. When she refused to see me again the following weekend, it occurred to me something had changed.

'What happened?'

'What're you talking about?'

'Something is wrong here.'

'Nothing wrong here. Business is good.'

'Really? Where are all the customers?'

'They're waiting for you to leave. *Gweilo* frightens them away. You better go—now!'

She never called me that. It stung. She faltered for a beat as if she understood what she had done. The moment was over, and she made wild brushing motions with her hands as if sweeping dirt out of her parlor.

'Get out. All us girls are busy!'

I backed away toward the parlor entrance and almost fell down the stairs. She chased me out onto the street. She gave me a speech that felt like something you would rehearse in your head or into a mirror.

'You need to go back to your nice comfy life and stop slumming it down here with the lower classes. Is this how you make yourself feel better about having so much more? Or are you looking for a bit of naughty adventure when you're bored with all your nice, clean, rich friends?'

'Don't you think I ask myself the same things? They tell me you're the wrong type.'

'I **am** the wrong type!'

People were looking at us, but I did not care.

'They say I should be with kids my age. They say it's not normal. They say it's not healthy. They say I could get in trouble.'

'I **am** trouble!'

'Why do I turn up week after week to a business with no sign, where strange men slink in and out? Why do I turn up every week to see someone I barely know? Who are you, Dolly? Who are you?!'

'You'll never know me!'

That shook me. I took a breath, long and deep, planted my feet, and bellowed.

'You'll die alone in that sad little flat! You deserve it!'

I saw the shock on Lily's face from an upstairs window. Dolly turned on her heel back up the stairs. She screamed at Cici to mind her own fucking business before slamming the door and shutting me out.

How did we get to this awful place? I had done nothing wrong, and yet, I felt guilty.

She needed something from me.

I put aside my school assignment and began painting a giant watercolor. It was the boudoir scene from Dolly's anteroom—*Dream of the Red Chamber*. I borrowed sable brushes from my tutor who liked to spoil me with such things. Everyone called her Ms Chen. I called her Madame Chen when nobody else was in the room, much to her delight. One of her brushes was an extra-fine *Series-7 Kolinsky* which I saved for detailing the face of the story's heroine, Lin Daiyu. However, I did not paint Lin Daiyu. I painted Dolly. I painted the girl I saw inside her who owed a debt of tears, like the heroine of the story. By the week's end, I commissioned an art shop in the city center to mount it on a frame of Red Toon mahogany. I saw a flash of recognition in the framer's eyes as he gazed upon my heroine. He told me he could read the story within my story, and he wished me good fortune.

I hauled the framed work all the way to the market and delivered it to Min, the strawberry lady. I asked her to pass it on to my anonymous benefactor who gave us free *Zhangji* strawberries. Min responded with a wink and a nod.

DOLLY

After I hung David's painting on my wall, I spent the whole night staring at it while lying on my bed in nothing but my panties. I loved that he chose watercolor rather than drawing as his medium. He was willing to learn a new skill to make this for me. There was a freedom and fluidity in his painting that was missing in other carefully constipated ink drawings of ancient romances. Most importantly, I found his message in Lin Daiyu's face. I saw myself in his painting as clearly as if it were a photograph of me. I sobbed until I was a disgusting mess.

One of my heroes, Eleanor Roosevelt, said it takes courage to love. Her words were all the more compelling since she harbored sapphic affection for her friend, Lorena. Eleanor said love's pain is the "purifying fire" felt by people who open their hearts completely. The fear of being hurt leads you to shut yourself away like a clam in a shell. The clam gives nothing, receives nothing, and shrinks until life is only "a living death". Her letters found in the 1970s revealed the secret love between these two women. One particular line stuck in my mind like an infectious ballad.

I want to put my arms around you and kiss you at the corner of your mouth.

I needed Eleanor's courage to make my move or move on.

Later that afternoon, I visited the Zhaojue Buddhist temple near the zoo. The temple was the most grandiose structure in our city. The saddle-shaped roofs, stacked one upon the other, were delightfully ostentatious. Gods and creatures carved in wood crawled all over the complex like the gargoyles of European cathedrals. I felt grounded among its many shades of earthen red.

All the usual pious bitches saw me coming. I was swathed in my most holy qipao dress. The garment was the color of the palest jade. The bitches gossiped behind their cupped hands. They shot glances at me while I bowed and prayed to that smiling fat cherub, Buddha. A monk passed me by, and we nodded to one another. I slipped some folding money into the donation box and selected a blank paper leaf from a wooden bowl for the wishing tree. I wrote on the leaf in heavy deliberate calligraphy.

Let me have this one.

his ancestral [illegible] Street. [illegible] photograph [illegible]

One of my heroes, Eleanor Roosevelt, said it [illegible] [illegible] compelling, since she had [illegible] Eleanor [illegible] [illegible]

[illegible]

[illegible]

Later that afternoon, I visited the [illegible] Buddhist temple [illegible] [illegible]

At the temple [illegible] I was [illegible] [illegible] calligraphy.

[illegible]

Five

DAVID

My stepmother played mah-jong every Wednesday evening with her gang of three old school friends. She bought a Hong Kong Style denim dress for the occasion. She called me into her bedroom to show me. Her waist was cinched tight by a chunky braided leather belt. Her thick wavy locks were teased into the most voluminous hairdo her salon ever conjured. Her final flourish was the reddest of red plump lips and matching heels. When I told her she looked seriously pretty, and all the other ladies would be jealous, she was pleased down to her toes. This was my standard response that made her happy.

Shortly after she left our apartment, Dolly called me on our telephone.

'Are you alone?'

'Yes.'

Say my name again.

'David, I just bought a new tape. Can I come over to hear how it sounds on your stereo?'

'Please. Yes.'

'Be there in an hour.'

She never invited herself to my home. Did she receive my portrait of her? Blood rushed to my face. I looked down at the comfy *Boy London* T-shirt and faded joggers I loved to wear around the apartment.

'I can't wear this!'

I raced into my bedroom and began pulling clothes out of my wardrobes. I chose a white T-shirt and Levi *501* jeans, just like Springsteen. I checked my look in the mirror, and something was missing. I recalled that Rob Lowe wore a button-down check shirt over his T-shirt in *The Outsiders.* He always appeared cool and relaxed in that film. Perhaps I could channel the same swagger? There were two check shirts in my wardrobe. Shit! Now I had to make a decision between two shirts!

DOLLY

Was it bad that I knew David's stepmother spent every Wednesday night playing mah-jong with her cronies? Was it bad that I knew she left home at the same time every time? Was it bad that I knew she wouldn't be back until late?

DAVID

An hour passed, and Dolly had yet to arrive. Perhaps I imagined her phone call in a dream? I was perspiring, which made me panic that I smelled bad. Chinese people will openly malign the body odor of Caucasians. I did not want to be that white guy. I raced into the bathroom to roll on some *Old Spice* deodorant.

There was a knock on my door.

DOLLY

I arrived early, but I wanted to knock on David's door later than I said I would. I wanted him to sweat for me. All the doors on his floor were decorated with images of the fire rabbit from the Chinese zodiac. The babies born in 1987 would be smart and headstrong. I would never be a mother, but I was a more than adequate lover. I leaned my back against the hallway, listening for the faintest sound of him through the wall. Was he feeling as anxious as me on the other side? I was about to take a leap of faith when I'd no faith left. Love takes too much courage for a reward too often fleeting. I was aching, horny, and defensive all at once. Was I about to make a fool of myself?
I knocked on his door.

DAVID

I opened my door to her. She wore my favorite qipao dress. The garment was as slick and as black as spilled oil. It fit her body like a wet glove. There was a diagonal slash of red embroidery in the shape of a phoenix that wound its way under her left breast, across her tummy, and curved over her right hip.

Whenever I met with Dolly, I always spent a fraction of time caught in her eyes. Surely, she was aware of her effect on me? Her eyes were a soft warm place, a home I had lost and then found again.

DOLLY

I avoided his eyes in more guarded moments, but not tonight. His eyes were jade-fire when he saw me. Sometimes they were gray when he appeared hurt or lost. They were the color of an emerald lake when he sang. I'd gladly spend the rest of my days watching his eyes change color.

DAVID

I showed Dolly the tape deck my father sent me from Japan. It was a *Nakamichi RX-505*. The deck was featured in a stylish Adrian Lyne film. I told her my father bought one for himself and one for me. I owned 104 cassettes, about a dozen of them were Japanese language tutorials. I stopped blabbering so she could say something—say anything—with that voice made of silk that bound me in its fibers.

'The only Japanese I know is *koi no yokan*. I'm told it's... the feeling you get when you meet someone, and you are going to... fall for them.'

Her right hand flailed and gesticulated in the air. She abruptly held it down with her left as if it were an unruly bird. I caught a blush rise to her cheeks before she turned away from me. Something was on her mind. I pulled focus back to my new toy.

'I wonder if I obsess with Japanese AV equipment because it is the only link I have with my father. See, he's an electrical engineer. He's also a venture capitalist in Japanese tech. I would say I miss him, but I don't recall enough about him to know what I'm missing. I know he's become fluent in Japanese. That's why I'm trying to learn it. One day, when we meet again, at least I'll have something to talk with him about.'

DOLLY

I wanted to tell him his father won't come back to him. His father was no longer a man, but an idea David was holding onto like a rosary to pray upon. Hope was to blame. The richer, prettier sister of Faith was to blame. It hurt me to witness his delusion. Yet, I was awestruck by how he fought against totally falling apart. One day Hope will leave him alone with a painful truth. It will be a wound he'll spend the rest of his life dressing. I wanted to wrap him in my arms and promise him it's going to be okay, he's still beautiful, he's still loved. I kept finding reasons to fall in love with this boy. I made an awkward attempt at levity.

'I know something that might put a smile on your face.'

I dug into my purse and drew out my identification document. This may seem like an absurd thing to do. However, there was a method to my madness. I handed my I.D to him. It included a terrible picture of me that looked like a prison mugshot.

'Glamorous, huh? And it has my real Mandarin name too, so you can understand why I prefer Dolly.'

I pointed out my name on the document.

Bik He.

It was written next to my date of birth.

10th of March, 1958.

My ulterior motive was that he'd see my age in black and white. I needed him to understand this fact. I wanted full disclosure before I made my next move. I checked his eyes for any sign of alarm or disgust and found none. All he showed me was his gentle smile. I found another reason to fall in love with him, another reason to want him.

DAVID

I did not think Dolly's I.D photograph looked any more or less terrible than mine. I was more interested in noting her birthdate. I often thought of a birthday gift for her. I asked Lily and Cici for Dolly's birthday, but it was a mystery to them as well. I was too shy to ask her directly. I committed her real name and her birthdate to memory. I smiled warmly and handed her papers back.

I was seriously awkward again. She seemed to be circling me. Her mood shifted gear. My heart was racing so fast I wasn't about to trust anything that came out of my mouth until I calmed down. I switched to a safe subject, my *Nakamichi*.

'The RX-505 is a unidirectional auto-reverse cassette deck.'

I pressed play. The bombast of *Bon Jovi*'s *Living On A Prayer* erupted from speakers that were the size of *jian gu* drums.

'When the end of the side is reached during playback, the assembly pops out the cassette, spins around 180 degrees, then the whole thing nips back into the deck, and keeps playing.'

I pressed 'Load' and the tape flipped sides in a whisper-quiet balletic motion. The iconic guitar riff of *U2*'s *With or Without You* marched from the speakers like an elegant love parade. I remembered her reason for the visit.

'Did you have a tape you wanted to play for me?'

'Later.'

There was something in her eyes I never saw before. Her eyelids were heavy like a film-noir actress. There was both a cool focus and an animal intent in her dilated pupils. She walked behind me and passed her hand across the back of my waist. I was beginning to enjoy her sudden and surprising familiarity with my body. Her breath tickled the back of my neck.

I babbled on, 'This unique auto-reverse function is remarkably quiet, and it takes only about one-and-a-half seconds.'

She was looking through all the framed photos of me scattered across the cabinets of our apartment. She picked up the red scarf I had not worn since I was in the *Young Pioneers of the Chinese Communist Party.*

'The deck will auto-reverse and auto-play until you make it stop.'

I wished my babbling would stop.

DOLLY

His stepmother must have curated a hundred photographs of David growing up, and various other childhood mementos displayed around his home. My eyes fell upon all of his trophies, framed awards, and cherubic baby snapshots until I spotted something quite useful.

I picked up his red *Communist Youth League* scarf. I twisted it in my fingers, stepped up close to his back, and wrapped the scarf around his eyes. I made sure he was blind, and then spun him around three times. He was so disoriented he must have forgotten about playing with his new toy. It was time for him to start playing with me.

'David, the safe word is Mao Zedong.'

'What's a safe word?'

'You say it when you want me to actually stop rather than pretending you want me to.'

'Why Mao?'

I laughed.

'Because nothing kills the mood more than that gross man.'

'Okay, Dolly.'

'Very good.'

I stopped and ejected *U2* from his *Nakamichi*, loaded my new tape in his deck, and pressed play. The familiar voice of George Michael strutted from the comically large speakers.

I Want Your Sex

DAVID

She slid her fingers deep into my hair and pulled my face close to hers. In the darkness of my blindfold, I heard her take a breath before pressing her lips to mine. There can be no deeper kiss than this. My blood was flooded with endorphins and I stumbled. She righted my body and supported me with hers. I instinctively reached for her hips and held her tight. I explored the perfect hourglass of her body under my hands in a way that was not possible with my eyes. There was suddenly a lot less room in my underwear now I had gotten so big and hard it hurt. I pushed my pelvis against hers. Could she feel what she was doing to me?

My practice kiss with Jolin did not prepare me for the ecstasy I found in Dolly's lips. The play of her mouth on mine filled me with a lush euphoria. She held my bottom lip between her teeth for a moment frozen in time before letting me go. She spun me around again to face a wall. She then slapped my bum like I was a horse saddled up for a race.

DOLLY

There was a full-length mirror adjacent to the door. I imagined it was for Mei Mei to check her outfit before she left home. I spun him around so he faced the mirror, but only I could see his reflection. I lifted his arms above his head, pulled the shirts off his body, and tossed them away. For the first time, I gazed at his naked upper body. He was so young, so hard and so soft all at once. His body was a welcome relief from the parade of porcine customers who were invariably covered in fat, gristle, and hair. He was everything I'd imagined, over and over again. I'd spent the last two years twisting and turning in the confines of the world's longest foreplay.

His skin was firm and smooth to touch with my jealous fingers. I felt awfully possessive and wanted him only for me. I gazed into the mirror and studied our reflection. My body turned toward him. My breasts were pressed into his torso, my hands wrapped around his waist. I savored the image like warm chocolate sliding down my throat.

I pushed his back to the wall, dropped his jeans and kicked them away. David's cock rose straight up. There was no wandering curve to the left or right. It was like a perfectly carved totem pole. The head of his cock was engorged pink with raw desire. I held his waist tight, lifted my knee, and pressed it firmly into the space between the base of his cock and his tightly packed young balls. I leaned into him. He drew a sharp ragged breath trailing off into a sigh. When all that pleasure hormone pooled into one throbbing mass, a small amount of pain morphed into a large amount of pleasure. My firm handling of his body was met by his soft caresses, blindly reaching out to touch me through the silk of my qipao dress. I ran a nail slowly up the length of his skin stretched tight around his cock, and then circled his plump head with all five nails. I paused for a beat, then pressed the tips of my nails a touch deeper into his delicate flesh. He cried out in pure unguarded pleasure. I loved how he surrendered to me. I loved how he trusted me to know what he needed. I traced my index nail along the apex-shaped lip of flesh under his head. This is the narrow place where all of his carnal feelings were focused. A squirt of pre-cum ran from the tip of his cock. I wiped it up with my finger and licked it clean. Yum.

I took a moment to admire his navel at the center of his smooth flat tummy. The doctor did such a beautiful job of his belly button when he was born. It was neat and cute, like a sexy dimple.

Then his fucking phone rang.

DAVID

My phone rang. You may assume this would break the spell. On the contrary, it only added to the multiple layers of pleasure. I heard Dolly stop the tape deck, pick up the receiver, and put it to my face. I took the phone in my hand. It was my stepmother.

'Hello, darling.'

'Hi, Ma.'

'Are you okay all by yourself?'

'I'm fine. Thanks for asking. Listening to my new stereo.'

'There are some Wontons in the freezer and leftover soup in the fridge for your dinner, darling.'

'Oh yes. Thank you for thinking of me. You're seriously thoughtful.'

DOLLY

I was sure his stepmother had the hots for him. That's why I fell to my knees in front of David and sucked his lovely cock while he spoke politely and patiently to her. I could feel him struggling to keep his breathing even and his voice calm. I was totally proud of him. I heard everything she was saying while I buried the head of his cock deep into the back of my throat without gagging. His eyes rolled back in his head when I flexed the muscles at the back of my tongue. I beat a rhythm like a heartbeat with every flex, sending pulses of pleasure I could feel under the palm of my hand that held his hip. I doubt his little friend Jolin would have managed such expertise.

Mei Mei's voice was high and whiney on the other end of the line.

'Don't wait up. I'll be home late. Bye bye, my beautiful boy.'

'Bye bye, Ma.'

Click.

I let his cock slide slowly out of my wet mouth and rose from the floor. I took the telephone receiver from his hand and put it back in its cradle.

My lips brushed his earlobes as I whispered into his ear.

'You must be hungry'

I wrapped one hand around his cock and tugged him toward an armchair. From what I could recall of his birthday, it was his stepmother's armchair. Good.

I resumed the music and turned up the volume a notch. The auto-reverse-and-play feature came in handy. We listened to the whole 49 minutes and 37 seconds of the album three times before we were finished that night. Teenage boys have stamina.

I returned to Mei Mei's armchair and took a moment to enjoy the sight of him, his vulnerability. He was such a good boy, he never once reached for his blindfold. I lifted my dress, stepped up onto the armchair, and planted my knees on either side of his body. I took a firm handful of hair at the back of his head and guided his mouth toward my pussy. It was hot down there and my inner thighs were slick and wet. Fortunately I arrived at David's without panties. One less thing to take off.

DAVID

Blinded, my remaining four senses were amplified. Her pussy was as delicious as the peach oolong bubble tea she was always sipping. I drank in the rich scent of her. She guided my hands to her smooth bare ass. I felt her muscles tighten as she thrust her pussy into my mouth. The sound of her hard and fast breathing was punctuated by the occasional squeal of delight. I felt myself sharing her joy as I gave it to her. My desire to consume her was matched only by her desire to be consumed.

DOLLY

After a while, my knees buckled from all the pleasure David was giving me. I climbed off, took his hands again in mine, and hauled him out of the chair. I kissed him deeply, enjoying the liquid taste of me on his lips. I led him to the big bed his father never shares with his wife.

DAVID

I was so intoxicated by everything I was feeling, it took me a minute to register that we had moved to my stepmother's bedroom. I caught the scent of Mei Mei's perfume mixed with Dolly's. My stepmother walked in a cloud of *Opium*. Dolly's scent was something newer—a heady, fleshy, dance of purple plum, tuberose, and perhaps cedarwood. I discovered many years later she wore *Poison* by Christian Dior to the very end.

Standing naked and blindfolded in front of her, I hesitated.

'Could we get in trouble? Is this legal?'

'The age of consent in China is 14. I think you've waited long enough.'

I followed the direction of her voice. I tentatively reached out my hands, found the line of her throat and moved toward the whisper of her breathing. My mouth found hers and my hands rediscovered the firm curve of her bum. She slapped me hard across my left cheek. I was startled, but my skin was flushed with unexpected pleasure. She resumed our kiss with such tenderness so the pain felt harder and the kiss felt softer by contrast. With both hands, she gently caressed the line of my jawbone. In one swift motion, she pushed me onto Mei Mei's bed.

DOLLY

I wanted to love him so deep it hurt to swallow my pride and admit this weakness. I wanted to flay his lovely young skin with my tongue made sharp with awful words. I wanted to throw him to a pack of Mongolian wolves only to rescue him and kiss his wounds.

He sat up in Mei Mei's bed with his back to the wall. I adored that he was both naked and blind. His rail-hard cock twitched in frustration. Perhaps he wondered which direction I'd attack him next? I crawled on the big bed softly so he wouldn't feel me come for him. I gave his cock a quick suck, eliciting a surprised yelp from the poor boy.

He spoke some whispered words I didn't quite catch. I moved closer. I held his face gently in my hands. My knees were planted on either side of him. My body arched over his lovely, tensed, prone body. My ear to his mouth.

Say my name. Say it.

'Dolly.'

'Yes?

'*Wǒ ài nǐ.*'

(I love you)

The blinding light of his words flooded all of my senses. A frightened part of me raised an alarm. I was scared, deliriously happy, and horny.

I peeled off my dress and guided his mouth toward my bare breasts. I doubt he was prepared for the shock sensation of my totally nude body. Another gorgeous burst of pre-cum spilled from the head of his cock. His mouth found my nipple and rolled and sucked the tense flesh between his lips, first one breast, then the other, leaving a liquid snail trail across my skin. His left hand found my hip and held it tight. Now that he'd found his bearings and where my body was located, he hooked his right arm between my thighs allowing me to rub my pussy into the crook of his arm. His right hand was planted firmly on my back. I felt held in place. My pussy glided across the tense flesh of his arm locked between my thighs, making him all slippery. My eyes rolled back as I enjoyed myself. He understood what I wanted, perhaps before I did. It felt as if he was remembering how to love my body rather than discovering it for the first time.

There was something else I wanted from him. I begrudgingly pushed his lovely mouth away from my nipples, grabbed his wrists tight, and held them fast against the wall behind him. I looked down at his swollen cock pointing directly, unerringly at me. My hair softly caressed his face as I gazed down at the hard evidence of how much he wanted me. I lowered my pelvis toward his lap. The sopping wet mouth of my pussy kissed the plump head of his engorged cock. I felt an urgent rhythmic throbbing from deep inside of him. I controlled it so he was not allowed to press himself any further than I let him. It took a great deal of my own self-control not to let this poor, tortured boy impale me.

'David, is this your first time?'

'Yes. It's that obvious?'

'Oh, *qīnài de*. You're going to thoroughly enjoy this, my love'.

I pressed my mouth to his with a tenderness clashing wonderfully with my vice-like hold on his wrists. I slid my vagina slowly over his grateful cock. He let slip the heaviest sigh I'd ever heard. It was beautiful.

I let go of his wrists. Now that his hands were free, he held my waist in his warm, heavy grip. I arched my back and planted my hands behind me into his thighs that were flexed so tight his flesh felt like marble. I moved my hips until I found the perfect angle where the head of his perfect cock would press into the perfect part of my vagina.

'Fuck yes, right there. Good boy.'

I looked down at his handsome diamond-shaped face, his eyes blinded, his brow furrowed. I imagined he was valiantly resisting the urge to blast ropes of cum inside me sooner than he wanted.

I kept rubbing that place inside of me with his cock. With each rock of my pelvis, a delicious tension coiled tighter and tighter in the pit of my belly. I'd barely enough time to process what was happening to my body. My peak was coming far sooner than usual. I was smashed by an orgasm as big and as terrifying as a tidal wave. My hips bucked toward him as I simultaneously sought out and tried to reel back from the searing white-hot pleasure. My head fell back, my mouth fell open, and I sprayed all manner of Mandarin profanities to the ceiling. I spared no thought for his upstairs neighbors, nor anyone else in the building. If his stepmother walked in on us, I'd have screamed at her to 'fuck off, I'm busy breaking in your son and cumming all over him!' I had never cum as quickly as I did that first time with him. Luckily I'd plenty more orgasms left in me for the rest of the night.

I wanted him to cum too. It didn't take a lot to drive him there. He threw his head back and cried my name as if it were his last breath. His hips snapped forward as his orgasm washed over him, tore through his body, and therefore into mine. I felt his cock twitching in my pussy and then a flood of hot liquid desire followed.

He sat bolt upright. I answered his shifting body by wrapping my legs around his waist and gently milking the rest of his cum into me as he recovered. I felt his breathing, deep, long, and hard into my shoulder. The honey smell of his thick glorious blonde hair filled my nostrils. I ran a fingertip along the curling folds of his ear. My other hand ghosted around his broad rippling back, my nails dragging over his flesh, digging deeper than I should.

I whispered into his ear, 'It's okay, baby. It's okay.'

It wasn't long before I felt him growing inside me again. I wanted to keep fucking him until I could feel him in my bones.

He was a lucky boy that night. I can't imagine what kind of amateurish fumbling would have occurred if any one of his little classmates broke him in rather than me. I knew how to bring him close to release, stopping at the edge, and make him hold his climax until I decided it was time to release it. If you want to ensure a man never dreams of greener grasses, then plant for him a field of flowers.

DAVID

When Dolly left my home, I took off my blindfold gradually so my eyes would adjust to the light. I discovered she had thoughtfully laid my duvet over Mei Mei's bed before we enjoyed all of that sex on top of it. The duvet was soaked in our cum and sweat, but my stepmother's linen underneath remained pristine.

I stood and studied myself in the Mei Mei's floor-to-ceiling mirror. Had I shed a skin to reveal a new one? I turned this way and that. Dolly left a mark on me, literally. I assumed she took a red felt-tip pen from my desk to write on my left bum cheek.

属于我.
(Belongs to me).

DOLLY

When I left David, I floated all the way home. As soon as I collapsed onto my bed, I doubled over in pain as if someone had punched me in the belly. I sobbed hard into my pillow, knowing how deeply I was in love. I was sure I would pay dearly for this gift. When a heart fills up, it can do nothing else but burst open. I fell asleep with tears drying on the sheets of my bed that was never made, in a room that's never clean nor tidy.

DAVID

Our school assignment caused a sensation when it was shown to the public at our school gallery. I made the drawings, and it was Jolin's role to present and frame the pieces as an installation. She did excellent work creating an intricate labyrinth of suspended panels and mobile frames paying homage to the alleys and laneways of Chengdu. Despite our success, Jolin was puzzled and somewhat annoyed by the subject of my drawings. I did not blame her, and I sincerely apologized for changing my drawings at the eleventh hour to something much more lurid. She appreciated, however, that my provocative vision pushed us over the fame edge.

Dolly briefly attended our exhibit dressed in the plainest clothes I ever saw on her body. Despite her efforts to remain non-descript, her white polo shirt and black poly-cotton slacks could not hide her Junoesque figure. Was she trying in vain to blend in with the many proud parents? Mei Mei could not stop smiling, right up until the moment she caught sight of Dolly entering the gallery.

Dolly understood my subject immediately. I spotted a blush rise to her cheeks as she recognised each drawing was a different part of her naked body. I had drawn the sweep of her waist and her navel, the arc of her throat and a fragment of her mouth, her fingers resting on the curve of her hip, the small of her back and the cleft of her bum, the underside of her breasts and a glimpse of her nipple. Since the night of our first adventure, I spent many more nights blindfolded with Dolly. Without the benefit of sight, I remembered every inch of her by feel and drew her body by touch-memory. I was able to conjure on the dark inner side of my eyelids her every line. This was the sum total of my love. It filled a room.

The inspiration of my drawings was meant to be a secret held close between the artist and his muse. It was meant to be a relationship nobody else would even begin to understand nor recognize. Nonetheless, I think Jolin saw it. As I introduced her to Dolly, Jolin's eyes ran from the head of my muse to her feet. Her gaze was slow and deliberate. I saw the color drain from Jolin's face. I was not blind to her affection for me, but I shoved her feelings into my blindside. Somewhere in a lonely part of my conscience, I understood my drawings would be a cruel revelation to Jolin. A woman had beaten this girl. The sound of Jolin's pain was drowned out by the cacophony of my love for Dolly. I did not care if the hurricane I let loose hurt anyone in its path.

Mei Mei and I arrived home late. She tossed her keyring with practiced precision into the small porcelain bowl by the door.

'You're not seeing that whore anymore.'

I smirked.

DOLLY

David was certainly not the first one to draw, paint, or photograph me. The last gentleman who tried was a *gweilo* customer from the U.S. He paid me only to sit for him while he earnestly swiped expensive *Schmin*cke oil paints all over a canvas. Eventually he approximated some kind of likeness of me. He painted no more than twelve pieces because, as he set me up for number thirteen, he tried to come on to me. The feeling was not mutual. He may have watched *The World of Suzie Wong* one too many times and assumed all his attention would cast a spell on this poor oriental girl. Ha! Last I heard, one of those paintings was hanging in MoMa or The Whitney—I could never recall which one. Anyway, I believed his style was derivative of Modigliani considering how much he stretched out my neck. On the other hand, my David derived from no one.

I thought of these things as I found myself staring at my beloved picture of Gia in the corner of our dressing room mirror. I heard she died, but Chinese news wouldn't say what killed her. I would have loved to enjoy tea with that beautiful rebel. There was a new picture cut from the latest UK *Vogue*. It was a black and white of Christy Turlington. The photograph was everything I adored about beauty and fashion in one image. Her ink-black dress barely clung to her body and showcased her bold, bare shoulders. Her hair was mussed. She stared down the lens as if daring her audience to do something daring. I checked my smolder in the mirror against the Turlington standard. There were several *Shiseido* liquid and pencil eyeliners in my red lacquer make-up case. These were gifts from a customer who bought them from the boutique in Ginza, Tokyo. I selected a kohl black pencil, sharpened it with a scalpel, and drew its darkness along the waterline under my eyes. For the first time in my life, I enjoyed having a good reason to look good. The monkey on my back had become a fixture before David. I'd forgotten how buoyant life could be when the monkey was gone, and I allowed myself to feel joy.

Three years had passed since love forced my hand and made me believe in it. I'm glad our feelings were slow to burn. Quick passions grow too fast for love to keep up with it. Love's not an answer to anything, but it's a witness. He saw me.

That particular night, I broke some bad news to Lily and Cici. I told them I couldn't join them at Karaoke or hot pot because I was going on a date. There followed an explosion of expletives from the girls. Those words, *I have a date*, had never been uttered from my mouth. The girls demanded I admit David was my boyfriend. I declined to confirm, but my smile betrayed me.

DAVID

I wanted to show Dolly a different side of me that night. I discovered the perfect dark gray worsted suit jacket and matching pants in my father's storage boxes. My body was grown enough to fit the collection of Giorgio Armani suits, shirts, and gloves he left behind. It was a safe bet he bought all of these designer clothes after seeing Richard Gere in *American Gigolo*.

I wore my jacket over a deep emerald dress shirt unbuttoned at the top. She told me she liked my mahogany leather shoes and matching belt. These were the things that completed my outfit.

She arrived at our rendezvous wearing the sweetest Sunday Church floral cotton dress and modest heels. Never have I seen, nor will I ever see, such a chaste outfit worn by Dolly. A fine gold necklace was threaded into a stone puppy dog charm laid across her throat. She played with her little jade dog with one hand while the other hand hid behind her back. Her dress was singing holy psalms, but her grin was all rock and roll.

'Hey, handsome. Looking for a good time?'

I met her grin with one of my own. I took her hand in mine. We set off through the neon Babylon of Chunxi Road. It was the place for late-night eats and whatever else you may desire. The place was alive with big appetites to fill and flashing neon signs of every color promising just that. Drunken friends and lovers clutched each other. A woman rode a bike between gaps in the crowd. Dozens of heart-shaped balloons were tethered to her frame. There was always something to buy and sell on The *Hundred-Year Gold Street*.

DOLLY

David opened the restaurant door for me. We stood before the tables and surveyed the space and its guests. It was a typical family restaurant with lots of filigree painted red and gold. The place was packed. Luckily he made a reservation. I ran my hand slowly down his back until I reached his ass and gave it a good squeeze.

Chinese culture has the sweetest taboos, which only made it more fun to break them. I relished every stolen glance shot our way as we were shown to our reservation by the maître d'. All eyes followed the old lady and her young boyfriend she snatched from a cradle. Some stared with veiled outrage, some with frank voyeuristic pleasure. They witnessed he and I express the most indiscreet of indiscretions, fleeting touches, whispered sweet-nothings, intimate secrets, and sitting far too close to be decent. I was betting I knew the most popular question on everyone's lips.

What the hell is she *doing with that white boy?*

We made sure there was no doubt we were lovers. I slipped my foot out of my shoe, pressed my toes against his crotch, and began the most civilized conversation I could muster.

'You know, my parents called me the other day.'

'Really? I hope you sent them my regards.'

He squirmed in his seat trying to regain a modicum of decency.

'Yes, indeed I did. They reminded me I'm 31 this year and it's way past time for me to grow up and be married off.'

I pressed my heel into his balls just the way he liked it.

'Oh, dear. What're you going to do?'

'Well, they've consulted an obscenely expensive matchmaker and they've got a lovely widower lined up for me. He's got a thriving pager business, which they say is the way of the future.'

David was playing with my bare toes under the table. He tickled the soles of my feet, and now it was my turn to squirm.

'Well, as long as he's lovely. I guess that's what counts.'

'There's the small matter of him being twice my age. However, I'm told beggars can't be choosers now I'm an old maid.'

We could barely stifle our laughter at our own shenanigans. The absurdity of my parents' involvement in my personal life at my age!

David was giving me a lecture about how pagers will be eclipsed by cellular phones. I'd made a grave error by mentioning anything regarding technology. I tuned out while he pontificated upon digital megatrends. The geek was lucky he was terminally pretty. I was tempted to shut him up with a kiss.

Our meal of *shuizhu yu* arrived like a delicious bounty to our table. This Szechuan dish is composed of tender fillets of carp. The fish is marinated, brined, coated, and slipped into a large brass pot of steaming broth with a thick layer of rich chili oil, bright red dried chilies, and mouth-numbing Szechuan peppercorns. You dip your chopsticks into the blend and lift the slices from their bath. The bite-sized pieces are drenched through the debauched concoction of flavors. If food was an orgy, this is what it would taste like.

Afterward, we fed each other slices of fruit for dessert. He especially liked the *Zhangji* strawberries.

'What's to become us, Dolly?'

'I think we're going to be great together.'

'Come closer.'

I moved forward in my chair.

'Closer.'

He pulled his chair back and patted his thigh. I left my seat and planted my ass in his lap. He reached out and traced his thumb along the pouty edge of my bottom lip, wiping away a faint spill of *Pinggu* peach juice. Until then, we'd yet to completely outrage someone. This was the last straw for a middle-aged woman at a table near the kitchen. She tut-tutted us before dragging her harried husband out of the restaurant. Awesome.

He paid the bill and we stepped out onto the street.

I said, 'I've a surprise for you, Mister Handsome.'

'Promise to never stop surprising me.'

'Knowing me, that is something I can guarantee.'

I looped my arm in his and took him on a journey to a building I know.

I possessed a key to open the lobby door of a stern-looking office building. It was built in the early days of the Republic when it served as the Department of Finance. Now it was used for things more fun. I threw the light switch and a bank of fluorescent tubes flickered into life.

DAVID

Dolly walked me down an apple-green hallway littered with tumble-weeds of dot-matrix paper and empty ramen packets. There was a vague smell of bureaucratic machinery ground to a halt long ago. As we walked past a couple of emptied offices, I spied a painter's easel here and a half-finished sculpture there.

'David, can you guess what this place is?'

'It feels like a building that's found a new job.'

'Yes. I have friends who share your new way of making art. This old building is their workshop. I would love to introduce you to the crew someday.'

I would eventually meet her friends but under the most extraordinary circumstances.

'Now, I want to show you my favorite part.'

DOLLY

My favorite part was the old-fashioned elevator. This grandiose slab of vintage mechanics had been designed with sensual art-deco flourishes and luxurious controls made of polished brass. The lift was built for a Shanghai hotel in the 1950s but was accidentally shipped to that Chengdu office block. He followed me inside the cozy, carpeted, wood-paneled cabin. I leaned my body into his and pressed the button behind him. The single tungsten bulb cast us both in a gorgeous retro light. My mouth hovered over his.

'I've always wanted to go down while going up.'

'What?'

I hiked up my dress and fell to my knees before him. My eager hands worked quickly at his belt and fly to set his cock free and into my mouth. He was already halfway hard, so by the time we were moving past the third floor. All the blood rushed to his engorged cock slick with my spit. I raked my teeth along the tender skin of his shaft, just the way he liked it. The slowly moving elevator produced a heavy, cavernous metal-on-metal humming as it took us higher.

The elevator door opened at the rooftop. I hopped to my feet and stepped out of the cabin, leaving him in a delirious mess. He haphazardly tucked himself back into his pants. The door almost shut on him before he pressed the button again and stepped out onto the roof with me.

From the rooftop, we enjoyed the most spectacular view of the gaudy lights and nocturnal action of Chunxi Road. From the moment I discovered it with my friends, my first thought was to share it with David. I walked to the waist-high wall at the edge of the roof to gaze upon the street below. Even from that height, you were still able to discern people hunting for food and fun in pairs or in packs. He joined me at the roof's edge and enveloped my body from behind. We fit like two pieces in a puzzle. We stood like that for long enough to absorb the moment. He pressed himself firmly against my ass, reminding me his arousal hadn't wavered since the elevator.

Nearby, there was a raised skylight on the rooftop. It was covered in thick reinforced glass and haloed by the building's interior light. He took my hand and guided me to sit on the glass.

'Take off your underwear.'

I complied.

DAVID

No blindfold this time. I wanted to see her. The skylight lent Dolly an ethereal glow tracing her every curve as she scooched further up onto the glass. A light breeze played in her hair. I told her,

'Now spread your leg—wide.'

I enjoyed telling her to do things she probably should not.

'Lift your dress. Show me your pussy.'

She was bare-naked from the waist down and I had not even taken off my jacket. I shot her a hungry gaze that burned the air between us. I wanted her to understand the full depth and breadth of how much I wanted her. I savored the moment, watching her watching me. She crooked her finger and beckoned to me.

'Come to mommy.'

I knelt before her and ran a trail of kisses along the inside of her thighs. She planted one foot into my shoulder, and steadied herself by splaying one hand across the glass. She used her other hand to grip a fistful of my hair and pull my mouth toward her pussy. I loved to take way too long to give her what she wanted. Her squeals and protests were a cruel delight.

'Stop it, I like it!'

I scooped up her bum with both of my hands and wrapped my mouth around her, sucking and licking her vulva. Her syrupy soft flesh felt as if I were running my lips over a White Yulan flower dipped in peach juice. She arched her neck and cried out in a voice hoarse with both agony and ecstasy.

'Eat me. Eat me. Eat Me.'

Her wanton dirty talk washed my brain with endorphins. Her shameless confidence flipped a main switch inside me. My cock was getting hard in an awkward position so that it ached in the confines of my pants. I wanted out of those clothes.

DOLLY

No blindfold this time. I wanted him to see me.

I thoroughly enjoyed having David between my thighs. He demonstrated a natural talent for licking my pussy. Probably because he was so into it. I held a fistful of his thick blonde hair and angled his tongue right where it needed to be. My hips clenched in a rhythm to match the quickening in my breath. He'd learned to be the most delightfully annoying pussy-tease. First, he got me so horny my brain turned to mush. Then, he let his tongue go still. I growled in frustration, roughly snapping my hips forward. At the height of my exasperation he got me so cranky I was almost sobbing. I felt like slapping his pretty face. Instead I scolded him.

'Stop being so cruel. Just lick me, suck me, do it!'

He complied. Then the humming began. He pressed his lips against my clit and hummed. The vibration caused a shudder to race up and down my spine. He lifted his lips from my skin and blew cool air up and down my hot pussy. He shifted his attention away to kiss and nip at my inner thigh, teeth scraping over my pale flesh. His warm hands roamed over the backs of my thighs and ass. He littered my skin with soft kisses and playful nips making me feel flustered that he wasn't paying the same attention to my clit. He smirked against the creamy white of my flesh.

'Bastard!'

I slapped him in the face. He answered my reprimand with more insolence. His tongue swiped only once across my vulva and I couldn't control the strangled cry escaping my mouth. After a lot of squirming, the teasing stopped. His deft tongue painted a path toward my cunt and found purchase on my clit again. I sunk into his mouth. I spoke to him in words I offered like a prayer.

'Eat me. Eat me. Good boy. My beautiful boy.'

With both hands, he lifted my ass off the skylight. His mouth seemed hotter and deeper from a higher angle.

My hands and feet were planted firmly on the glass. A panicked thought tugged at the last part of my mind that was still working. What if the glass breaks? As usual, the fear shifted my pleasure into overdrive. The more his tongue caught right under my clit, the sharper my hips jerked until a glow in my belly grew into the blinding white heat of an orgasm that set everything on fire.

The raw sensitivity caused by my first orgasm blended deliciously with the pleasure of my second, and then my third. Each time, my whole body violently spasmed. My feet beat a staccato against the glass, and my teeth clenched and rattled in my mouth. If I were more sober, I'd have been embarrassed. It probably looked like some kind of psychotic seizure. However, in those moments of pure surrender, I was more than happy to embarrass myself in front of him. Maybe I'm as much of a masochist as I'm a sadist. Every time I fell apart, I was rebuilt in his arms. When I was finally too exhausted to find another climax, I cried absent-mindedly. It was disarming how he made me feel so disarmed.

As I calmed my body, he softly lapped up all the wet that ran down my thighs. Once I began to think straight again, I demanded,

'Kiss me. Kiss me. Kiss me.'

Our lips were locked. I was drunk on the taste of him and I together in my mouth. I hooked my thighs tight around one of his legs and rubbed my pussy against his thigh. One of my hands played with his hair. The other rubbed his cock through his pants with an urgency unbecoming of a lady.

'Enough! Fuck me.'

He stepped back from me and paused for a moment, as if for effect. Off came his jacket. He took far too long to undo each button of his shirt. Inch by inch, I enjoyed the slow reveal of the broad expanse of his chest and broader shoulders. He finally peeled the deep emerald shirt from his body. I bet he chose green because he knew damn well it would make his eyes pop. Those jade-fire eyes were trained on mine. His body had developed beautifully since that first day he sat in my chair. There were muscles where there were none before. The next thing to take off was his shoes. My boy was astute enough to take off his socks before his pants. If you don't, then it looks funny when you're naked except for the argyle socks your stepmom bought you. His pants fell to the ground and he kicked them away. He took a moment to let me look at him in the moonlight as the high breeze tousled his long hair. His backbone was straight, shoulders back, tummy flat, and his cock pointing skyward.

Yes, there **is** a god.

I sighed and played with myself.

He approached me and arched over my body. I snatched his waist between my thighs. He pressed his cock against my vulva and rested his forehead against mine.

'Beg me.'

His voice took on a husky bass oozing with animal intent. I'd never begged for anything, even when I was a starving child. I hesitated, then uttered a single word.

'Please.'

That single word was the loneliest sound that ever fell from my mouth. Nevertheless, he seemed to be waiting for something more from me.

'Please. I want you. I want you inside me so bad it hurts without you.'

That's what he needed to hear. He nuzzled his cock into my grateful pussy. He fit so snug inside me. It was where he belonged.

'Lover... ride me.'

I'd taught him this lovely scooping motion with his pelvis so he rubbed the head of his cock into the right part of my vagina. A particularly hard thrust made him gasp and then hiss.

'Oh, *fuck*, yes!'

It occurred to me I'd never heard him curse. His sudden profanity turned up the heat. I wanted more.

'I want to hear more filth come out of that pretty mouth of yours.'

He seemed to ponder this for a beat.

'I'm gonna fill you with so much cum. I'm gonna watch it run out of you like a river.'

'Young man, what would your parents think if they knew you were hiding such a disgusting imagination?'

He laughed and picked me up. My ass nestled in his hands, my legs wrapped around his waist. He brought me over to the edge of the rooftop against the waist-high wall, spun me around, lifted my dress from behind, and nudged my legs apart with a swift motion of his feet. I thoroughly enjoyed how he pushed me around like a fuck-doll, one hand on my waist, the other piloting his cock up my vagina. Once he was home safe, it was his turn to grab a fistful of my tresses. Every time he thrust himself up inside me, he pulled my hair at the scalp, and claimed me over and over again. His body caged mine. He spoke more freely than any other time we'd made love. He said abstract things that only made sense in the moment.

'You didn't know what you were getting yourself into. Caught up in something you weren't looking for.'

'Yes.'

'You should have known this. I think you knew. Secretly, you knew.'

'Yes.'

'Tell me everything you want me to know.'

'I want to.'

'I can't guess the things you're thinking.'

'David?'

'Yes?'

'*Wǒ ài nǐ.*'

(I love you)

There, I said it.

I held fast to the wall and pushed my ass hard against his body. Standing so close to the edge of the rooftop got me more wet. It turned me on that the crowds on Chunxi Road could see me getting railed from behind if they ever chose to look up.

I imagined all those people looking at us in the restaurant. I imagined being naked in front of them. The image brought wave after wave of pleasure crashing onto my shore. Among the faces from the restaurant, I thought I spied a familiar one. Was it someone who'd bring danger? Fear gripped my chest. My breath was caught, panicked like a bird trapped in a room. In that terrifying moment, my body released the mother of all climaxes. A floodgate opened in my body. I drowned in a stupor of pleasure. I felt David react to my body, and convulse into his own climax. He emptied everything he had inside of me. I screamed his name into his mouth as it closed over mine and we split the night with a kiss.

On the other side of the rooftop was my friend's unfinished, but larger than life, sculpture of Icarus. He was falling to Earth after flying too close to the sun. His mouth, permanently twisted into a rictus of surprise carved into stone.

I could always rely on David to walk me home. Our clothes were dirty and torn in places. Neither of us cared to acknowledge the damage. We arrived at my 1930s walk-up flat where I was sure many single people dwelled before me. Did they all find love and move out? Was I hanging onto my single room and my single bed because it demanded so little of me?

The Go Master, Li-Jie, was teaching a student in his school under my flat. His patient tutelage filled me with awe. The walls of his school were covered in framed photographs and watercolor paintings. I recognised him in a few pictures. We nodded a greeting to each other. His eye lingered on David.

He and I stood for a moment at the bottom of my stairs. A single bare bulb in the narrow stairwell gave only enough light to find my key.

'Good night, Dolly.'

'Sweet dreams, *qīnài de.*'

One last soft kiss, barely touching my lips. I then turned and climbed upstairs into my flat.

Who was that face at the restaurant?

DAVID

There was a storeroom in the back of the art department in Chengdu University. It was filled with arcane artifacts whose origin and use were largely a mystery. I spent a lot of time exploring and solving these mysteries in that small musty room lit by a cool fluorescent light tube. That is how I discovered the *Rand* Graphics Tablet from 1964. It was the first device allowing the artist to draw shapes with a stylus on a printed circuit so they would appear on a computer screen. This antique of American computer design had absolutely no business being in the storeroom of a Chinese school. There was a rumor it was originally used to convert Mandarin characters to English for visiting academics. With a little help from the head of the electronics department, I was able to cable it up to a personal computer. I was imagining all sorts of things possible with the *Rand*.

DOLLY

Fatty Dong rolled his metal balls in his hand with such enthusiasm it was clear a bad moon was rising. He stood in my parlor with news.

'I just wanted to let you know your friend in the Tax Ministry has disappeared.'

'Oh, that's unfortunate for him.'

I tried to be nonchalant as I busied myself folding towels. This task was therapeutic for me when dealing with dickheads. Nevertheless, a seed of panic grew inside a forgotten corner of my mind.

'I am afraid The Party threw your friend in a hole then threw away the hole, my dear.'

'You and I both know people don't disappear forever.'

He chuckled mirthlessly.

'Yes, yes, but until then, I'll be auditing your accounts to make sure they are square with all this good business I know you're enjoying. My watchers are still watching you, my dear.'

In the worst timing in the history of time, David walked through my parlor door and met my boss. Fatty said something that crawled up my spine like a rat.

'Ah, and here is the young boy who's been preoccupying my employee so much for so long! Did you enjoy your dinner together on Chunxi Road?'

The familiar face at the restaurant. The watchers were watching. We were being watched.

I gathered all my composure.

'David, this is Fatty Dong.'

'Nice to meet you.'

David extended a cordial hand which was not taken because my boss's right hand was busy with his balls. David instantly picked up what was going down. He was a remarkably old 18-year-old after all. His response was both sexy and reckless.

'Your name is Fatty Dong? Seriously?

'Yes, boy.'

'And you're okay with that?'

I felt a spark of pride in my David. For one glorious moment, Fatty's machismo machine ground to a halt. He then collected himself.

'Well, I'll leave you two for your appointment.'

He stepped close to David. Fatty's words prickled my skin like ants.

'Have fun. I hear all her customers say she's quite talented. Awfully popular, my Dolly.'

He shot David a smile dripping in slime and left my parlor, taking his stink with him.

'I'm sorry about him, David. He's a legend in his own mind. He believes everyone is trying to rip him off. Maybe we are, but that's only because he's a dick.'

David's laughter was warm and broke the tension nicely. He took my hand in his.

The villain of every story imagines himself as the hero of his own personal narrative. Will Fatty Dong be the villain who ruins my happiness? Who or what will be my opposing force during the peak of my story arc? Was David the hero in my story, or was I the hero in his? Were we living a parallel narrative sharing the same story? The idea kept me warm against cold thoughts.

DAVID

On February 5th, 1989, The Beijing National Art Gallery opened the *Avant-Garde* exhibit. Jolin and I were honored to be invited to present our installation. As we rode the bus to the capital, we discussed the latest big issue. There was a new disease called AIDS. Until then, Chinese people were told by the Communist Party that AIDS was a Western affliction, like heroin addiction. That year, an AIDS outbreak was discovered among heroin users in Yunnan. China was waking up to what the rest of the world was already learning.

We arrived at the gallery excited to set up our installation. There was a wonderful camaraderie among the 186 kindred artists. Unfortunately, the exhibit was shut down by the police two hours after it opened. One of the artists, Xiao Lu, shot her artwork with a small pellet gun. This became known internationally as *The Gunshot Event*. Xiao was interrogated by the police for three days, after which she fled to Australia for a decade.

There was something ominous in the air. Like a green sky before a storm of hailstones. We would all be damaged.

DOLLY

While David was at the exhibit with that little girl, I met my friends at the opera. This particular opera house was far too hidden for the tourists to find. That's why we loved it. Henry and Jūn were my oldest surviving friends. I'd known this couple since The Communist Party's famine almost killed us.

Empty bird cages hung from the high ceilings. I was reminded that The Party had decreed for a brief period that sparrows were one of The Four Pests to be eradicated. After killing most of them, it was discovered these harmless birds were important for the environment. Our rice paddies suffered. The Party shifted their policy to a war on bed bugs.

My friends and I made a decision that evening at the opera that would change our lives more than we bargained for. Our fate was sealed. The moment was clinched by the ancient performance we enjoyed together.

The actress was facing our row, looking directly at us. We were caught in the trap of her gaze. Her costume was as brilliant and colorful as an elaborate fishing lure. Her regal headdress boasted two long, smooth pheasant tailfeathers. She stroked and preened them like a cat. But it was her mask upon which we were fixated. The Szechuan Opera was where we enjoyed the art of *bian lan*, or magical face changing. With one barely perceived gesture, her mask disappeared, only to reveal another mask expressing a new guise or emotion. She switched from comedy to tragedy in a way the ancient Greeks would have envied. The actress played out her pantomime, revealing one unique mask after another. Sometimes she would feign a change. We would hold our breath anticipating a new mask, but she tricked us, and her face remained the same. My friend, Jūn, was an enthusiastic opera fan. She saw the melodrama of people and politics writ large in the flurry of faces.

Each face slipped into a hiding place as another slid into view. Eventually she ran out of masks and so concluded her performance. Her final true face was revealed (or was it?). She smiled at us, bowed, and then returned to the dark behind the curtain. The house applauded.

The place fell into a quiet murmur, and I began to hear the song of Henry's cricket. My friend carried a live cricket in a small wooden cage. Sometimes it was in his coat pocket. That night it was on our table. The ancient secrets of cricket keeping were suppressed by The Party. It was deemed an antiquated distraction. However, a dozen secret markets flourished in the 1980s. *The times they are a-changin*, said an American folk singer whose music was banned from China.

Jūn smiled at Henry and took from her faux leather handbag three white bandanas, each with "Democracy Now" written on them in Mandarin.

DAVID

My new Beijing friends wrote me letters about something extraordinary that was happening in our capital. Students from the Central Academy of Fine Arts built a statue of liberty made from white plaster and Styrofoam. They were bold enough to plant it in Tiananmen Square facing the giant portrait of Mao Zedong. It was delivered as night fell, in three huge segments carried on tricycle carts. As the sun rose, a crowd filled the square to welcome the statue. People from all walks of life cheered and stared in awe. Why choose a symbol from America? Most of my friends had studied there and they understood the human rights they were missing when they returned to China.

The only report in the *People's Daily* about the statue was the government order to take it away. The paper called it an abomination, and decried, "This is China, not America."

A student protest was well underway. Hong Kong was still a free country in those days, so they sent the protesters a shipment of tents. Now they could sleep in the square overnight in comfort. The tents were pitched in neat rows near Mao's mausoleum where his dead body lay. One friend on the scene wrote that the bright red and blue tents cheered up the place.

The Communist Party responded by surrounding the capital with hundreds of thousands of soldiers. The moderate party chief, Zhao Ziyang, who backed economic reform, expressed some sympathy for the student demonstrators. He was placed under house arrest. By May 19, The Premier declared martial law. The soldiers moved in to the Square.

DOLLY

Walking in public together is something most couples enjoy with a light heart. I, on the other hand, invited scandal when I was seen in broad daylight walking hand-in-hand with a young white boy. People gawked at us. A man took a long hard look at David as he squatted over the gutter and picked his teeth with a stick. A mother clutched at her coat and wrinkled her face at me. She shuffled her teenage daughter to the opposite side of the road.

I liked it.

It was David's 19th birthday, and I took a day off to walk with him along the Fuhe River. We were looking for someone selling tanghulu, a sweet street snack we enjoyed. It was a winter Beijing treat so we didn't always find it in our city. Tanghulu was made by skewering a row of bright red hawthorn fruits and dipping them into a warm sticky sugar syrup which cooled into a crisp coating around the tart chewy fruit. The vendors pierced the skewers into a straw broom-head. That's how they carried them through the streets to sell. David always made sure there were no seeds in the fruit because he knew I liked it that way.

He brought along the gift he'd received from his father. It was a *Polaroid* camera he saw in a James Bond movie. As usual, his father bought one for himself and one for his son. As usual, I had to listen to a complete technical breakdown of the entire fucking gadget.

'The *Spectra* uses glass lenses rather than the plastic ones used in the regular box-style *Polaroids*. Plus, the film has a wider, more cinematic format than the regular 600 film.'

All I heard was *blah, blah, blah.*

'Plus, it has this seriously cool double-exposure setting. Check out the electronic display! See? Right here.'

He handed me the camera. I squinted at the LCD screen trying to fight against my bad eyesight. He gently suggested something.

'Use your spectacles.'

'What spectacles?'

'The ones you hide from everyone.'

I blushed to the roots of my hair.

'How did you know?'

'I see the way you squint at things.'

Did I squint?! I begrudgingly took my big ugly glasses out of my bag and put them on. Everything snapped into focus. I looked at him.

'Oh my God, you're hideous. I can't believe I'm dating you.'

He laughed and reached into his backpack and took out the same thick dorky spectacles as mine.

'Turns out I've the same affliction. My doctor figured out I need glasses to read now.'

He spun the *Polaroid* around toward our faces and took a photograph of us both. I believe this is called a *selfie* these days. The Bond version of the *Polaroid Spectra* shot a deadly laser beam. Fortunately, this one did not. Instead, this camera did something more magical. It clicked, whirred, and spat out an instant photograph. I'd never seen a *Polaroid* picture develop before. The image rose to the surface like daylight breaking through a milky fog. The colors were painterly as if the device was less of a camera and more of an impressionist. The image that resolved before my eyes was a lovely photograph of a couple of four-eyed nerds.

I begrudgingly let him take another *Polaroid* of me managing a smile while I sat in a rickshaw. He insisted I wear my glasses. Perhaps I should have been more grateful he wanted to preserve those moments on those curious rectangles of film. Photographs of our loved ones were confiscated from us during the Cultural Revolution. I wished David's magic camera would spit out all the photographs stolen from me. Within a month he'd covered the space above his bed with one-hundred *Polaroids* of me. This totally annoyed his stepmother.

Good.

We strolled along the river some more. Walking and talking with him was as satisfying as flying a kite, as if harnessing a natural force tethered to us. We were compelled to look up at the sky in wonder. A pair of bailu chased each other through the air above the river. One bird dove westward under the Anshun Bridge while the other swooped past its partner toward the east. I wondered how long this dance played out after we'd gone.

There was a question burning the tip of tongue since David and I began this thing.

'Don't you ever get jealous? ...of my customers?'

'No. I can see you're different with me.'

'How would you know? You're not even in the room with me when I'm working.'

'Since the day we met I've been observing you.'

All of this "observing" he was doing was both endearing and annoying.

'Oh really, Mister Detective?'

'I see you greet your customers. See you walk them out.'

'Still, you don't know what I am like behind the door.'

'It can't be much different behind closed doors. You give them a mask, like an opera mask. You don't bother with all that theater with me.'

The bastard was right.

'Acting is tiring work. I don't want to work when I'm with you.'

'I can see you aren't working when you're with me. Besides, I'm far better looking than any of your customers.'

He laughed. I hit him

'You're so cocky. Who said you were good looking?'

'I see you checking me out, dirty old lady.'

I hit him again, harder.

'*Shén jīng bìng*!'

(Mental case)

I admitted something and immediately wanted to reel the words back into my stupid mouth.

'I get jealous of you.'

'Jolin, right?'

I was totally outraged. How dare he notice my jealousy of his little school friend?! I said another stupid thing.

'That fucking little bitch better back the fuck off!'

People on the street turned around at my cursing. I was beyond caring. David laughed again! I smacked his ass.

'I'm not joking.'

'Oh, I can feel that.'

His laughter was demoted to a smirk. For fucks' sake, I was on a roll with stupid confessions!

'I'm jealous during the day, but at night I think about it, and it turns me on. That's totally messed up, right?'

'I have messed up feelings, too. Talk to me.'

'I picture you two together... kissing. It makes me angry, but also... hot.'

He walked closer to me, so our shoulders brushed. He held my hand tighter and leaned in to listen closely.

'Is that all?'

'You're fucking her like a boss, and I'm telling you how to do it.'

'Are you there with us?'

'Yes, but no. I don't know. I know I'm in control of the thing.'

The sky was growing dark, and so were my thoughts. I looked around to make sure no one could hear me and whispered stupid thing number-three into his ear.

'Oh, David. I want to watch you with someone else. I know of a way. Let's do it tonight before I change my mind.'

DAVID

We rode a smoky old State bus back to her flat. I could tell she was more anxious about showing me her place than anything else we were about to do. She seemed to procrastinate at the foot of her staircase. I fiddled with the overnight bag I packed. She stared at her keys as if she were looking for answers in them. A decision seemed to have been made. In one swift movement, she turned and powered up the stairs two at a time. She barged through her doorway before I had the chance to catch up. I found her standing there in the middle of her room. She seemed to be appraising the awful mess she made of her space. Her eyes rested on me.

'Okay. Are you in?'

'I am.'

'Then say you love me.'

'You're the only one I deserve. I love you, Bik He.'

My mouth went dry at the sound of her real name from my lips.

'You see me for me.'

'I do.'

'Then help me clean up this messy girl's room.'

I was sent downstairs to the Go Master to borrow cleaning supplies. I returned with a giant rubbish bag, a straw broom with no handle, an old tin bucket filled with hot soapy water, a mop with a head made of shredded rags, and a fistful of incense to burn because Dolly's room smelled like her feet after a long walk.

DOLLY

We filled a big hessian rubbish bag with things I should have jettisoned from my room ages ago. The flat was now clean and inviting enough for what we had in mind. I snuck David into the building's communal bathroom for a well-earned shower with me. He seemed quite practiced at showering with another woman, and I bet I know why (fucking Mei Mei). We washed away the day.

I made a phone call.

One hour later we were choosing a table at *The Red Panda Restaurant* nearby. The cook shouted hello to me from her kitchen. David was about to find out she made the greatest *gong bao chicken* he will ever taste. The sauce was the perfect blend of sweet, sour, and sticky.

Anxiety crawled up my spine. I had no rational reason to be anxious, but there it was. We were both dressed beautifully in matching outfits. David was wearing a jet-black button-down shirt. The collar was high and sharp. It complimented all those soft blonde tresses falling to his shoulders. He looked like a handsome gangster with a golden heart from the movies—but nothing like the real Triad gangsters who were actually smelly, greasy monkeys. I had to stop looking at him, for fucks' sake! He was cocky enough already. As we sat down, I caught him checking out my ass in my body-contoured black velveteen dress. I gave him a wink.

'Checking out the merchandise?'

He blushed. It was nice to know I could still surprise him. I chose a seat with a clear view of the doorway. There was only us and another couple dining in. It was late and the restaurant was serving mostly take-away by then.

Lily walked into *The Red Panda* right on time. She was reliable to a fault.

'Hi, guys.'

David stood up to pull a chair for her. I was blessed with considerate and beautiful company. Lily had changed out of her work qipao and into the short soft-pink dress I told her to wear. It was one of mine I kept in my wardrobe at the parlor. It was the same shade of pink she painted on her nails. She'd let her hair down and it cascaded in combed-out waves over one shoulder. Her baby-face was rouged with my blush and her lashes were made plump with my mascara. She looked like a dessert made of girl.

'So glad you could join us.'

'I'm so happy you asked me to join you! How was your day off, Dolly?'

'I went on a date with some guy.'

'Oh really? Is he handsome?'

Both Lily and I grinned at David.

'Well, he certainly thinks so.'

We all laughed and then ordered three dishes and a pot of rice to share. Everything was delicious, both the food and the company.

The waitress cleared our table.

'Do you want anything else, Dolly?'

'Yes. May we have three small cups of *Gujing Gongjiu* liquor?'

'Of course. I will put it on your tab.'

I smiled. This was a tab I never needed to settle. The waitress was in on the secret.

'Thank you, Annie.'

David shook his head.

'Is there anyone you don't know?'

'I know the owner, or, I know what he likes.'

Lily and I shared a giggle.

'So why did you two invite me? Why was I invited and not Cici as well?'

'David and I wanted to get to know you more. You're such a quiet little thing.'

Annie returned to our table with a squat black ceramic bottle embossed with gold letters. She laid out three fine porcelain cups and filled them with a liquor which smelled of orchids. *Gujing Gongjiu* was distilled using water drawn from a well in the Anhui Province. It was as pure and absent of color as crystal. We raised our cups and made a toast.

'*Gānbēi*!'

The mellow taste bloomed on my tongue. The spirit carried hints of cinnamon and a sweet-fire mouth-feel afterward. We smiled at each other as we swallowed our drinks in one shot. Lily's gaze lingered a little longer on my David.

We were loitering on the street outside the restaurant (a crime punishable in China, carrying a sentence of forced labour). We were all drunk, and that's the best time to gossip.

'Lily, did I tell you David's stepmother has the hots for him?'

'Of course she does! He's... you know... hot.'

She gave David a smile a little loose around the edge from liquor. He returned the smile and held it longer than was decent. Why did this excite me to no end? A familiar warm feeling spread its fingers through my tummy.

'Dolly, stop gossiping!' he cried in mock outrage.

'David, did I tell you Lily was in love with a customer, but he moved away?'

'Dolly, stop gossiping,' she cried in mock outrage.

'She used to look at him the way she's looking at you right now, David.'

'Dolly!'

Lily swiped her long pink claws at me, but I ducked. Her scowl was followed by a smile.

Passers-by snapped their heads back at the commotion we caused. I shepherded my companions down a deserted side street with fewer streetlights and more shadows. Lily opened up about her lost object of affection.

'He was not a good kisser, though.'

'Hear that, David? "Not a good kisser." What a shame. Not everyone is a good kisser like you.'

David shoved his hands in his pockets, hung his shoulders, and feigned some semblance of humility.

'I am?'

'Yes, you are. Come over here.'

Lily's eyes darted between the two of us. A hungry little smile played at the corner of her mouth. I grabbed David by his fancy shirt and pulled him toward a deep pool of shadow between two shops.

'Lily, you better come over here too so you can see how it's done.'

She looked up and down the street before joining us, cozied up in our darkened nook. His hands were all over my hips pulling me toward him. My hands were down the back of his pants feeling his ass. We pressed our noses together, smiled, and then kissed like we were the first and the last lovers on Earth. I opened one eye and saw Lily wearing the same syrupy gaze I saw in myself when I ogled David. I reached out my hand and held hers. David and I slowly parted lips. I took one step back and squeezed Lily's hand in my own.

'You're welcome to kiss my boyfriend.'

Boyfriend.

I enjoyed the claim I made over him when I used this word. David held out his own hand to Lily. She took it timidly. We held both her hands and all of her attention.

'So, you mean like the four-hands massage we do with customers, but kissing instead?'

We never kissed our customers. I suspected it was a long time since she kissed a man. It was a long time since I'd juggled more than one person outside of work.

'David's not a customer. Tonight, he's our lover-boy.'

That phrase seemed to unravel us. She and I shared a conspiratorial giggle. Our lover-boy gently pulled her toward him. He placed her hand on his chest and smiled at her. I wondered if she felt his pulse through her palm. She trailed that hand down his torso. She took away her other hand from mine and placed it on his hip. I put my hands on the small of her back and gave her a gentle push so her breasts brushed against his chest. I held her there. She wasn't wearing a bra because I bullshitted her it wouldn't suit the dress. She was high-beaming him so bad. He'd soon find out hers were the most succulent nipples I'd ever seen. He brushed a stray hair from her face with fingers that touched her earlobe, trailed her jawbone, and finally rested on her little chin. He took a small breath and pressed his soft lips over hers. I could feel her body buckle in my hands. Her fingers made claws and she was clumsily pulling his shirt from the confines of his pants. As soon as he was untucked, her hands swooped underneath his shirt. I bet she was discovering how firm, smooth, and warm he felt under there. I was transfixed watching them kiss. His lips were addictive, and I wondered if I'd made a mistake by sharing my narcotic with her.

Some old bag on the upper floor slammed open her window and began shouting at us. She threatened to pour a bucket of water on our party if we didn't take it elsewhere. So, we ran away laughing like children down the street to take it elsewhere.

My room smelled more agreeable since we burned incense of bergamot and ylang-ylang. All my books were neatly stacked in waist-high towers against the walls. The bouquet of red carnations David bought me so many moons ago was hung and dried over the head of my bed. My sheer white voile curtains were neatly tethered open so anyone could see inside if they so desired.

David was the last to enter. As soon as he closed the door behind us, he kicked off his shoes and tore off his shirt so fast even *my* head snapped back. All this self-confidence was both sexy and annoying. He needed discipline. I slapped him so hard on the ass he fell into the arms of Lily who immediately wrapped her lips around his nipple. She hooked her fingers into his belt and hauled him closer. He winced when she sunk her teeth into his flesh. I knew he liked it because I'm the one who taught him to like it. He answered her cruelty by fisting her hair and messing up her carefully combed waves without giving one shit.

He looked at me and I could tell he understood what I wanted to see. I desired a hierarchy with me at the top and Lily at the bottom. I took a seat in my rosewood chair. I ran my hands over my breasts through the velveteen of my dress and enjoyed the show.

He leaned his back against the wall. Her lips tore away from his nipples and gravitated toward his mouth. He raised her dress, raised his knee, and wedged it up against her pussy. She rubbed herself against his thigh like a bitch in heat. He bit her lower lip and held it, precisely the way I do. Her brow furrowed and then she sighed when he finally let go.

He picked her up, cradled her in his arms, and laid her down on my bed. He seemed quite good at this for whatever reason. I wanted him to cradle me as well. I would ask him later.

She propped her head upright with my pillows and stuck her right high heel into his chest. He grabbed her right ankle, tore off the shoe, and flung it into the corner of the room with his shirt and shoes. Then he shoved her bare toes into his mouth and gave them a big, noisy, wet suck. She squealed right on cue. He tore off her other shoe, grabbed both of her ankles in his right fist, and lifted her ass off the bed. I could see from across the room her panties were soaked through. He used his other hand to slowly peel her panties away from her ass, over her thighs, her calves, and her feet. He paused and stared into her eyes for a moment, smiled, and then abruptly threw her panties in her face. A snail-trail of her own wetness gleamed across her bottom lip. She yelped in shock and delight and then chucked her wet panties into the corner along with her heels. He took an ankle in each fist and grazed his teeth along each of her calves in turn. I could see he was building a journey along her body that would conclude with his tongue on her clit. The anticipation was driving her crazy as he took his sweet-fuckin-time getting to the point. I could sympathize with her frustration because he enjoyed frustrating me as well. He hooked his hands behind her knees and spread them apart. He painted wet lines along her thighs with his tongue leading toward her pussy. She was losing patience, so she pulled her dress (my dress) above her waistline and played with herself in-lieu of his mouth. That was cheating. He pushed away her eager hands and laced his fingers in hers. He took a moment to lock eyes and grin at her. The bastard was enjoying watching her squirm. She should have hit him. I would have hit him—hard. He pulled an elastic band from his wrist and tied the lion's share of his hair behind his head into a messy bun. He dived down between her thighs and drew a slow circle with his tongue around her pussy without committing to placing it where she wanted it most. She shifted around like a brat indulging in a tantrum. Finally, his mouth enveloped her pussy and her whole body went limber. The fingers of his left hand parted the hood of delicate flesh away from her clit. Two fingers of his right hand disappeared into her vagina. I imagined he'd be rapidly switching those fingers together inside her. I loved it when he did that to me. Her body made graceful waves while she absently touched his face between her thighs. She began to babble.

'I always liked you.'

'Why did you like me?

'You're so beautiful. You have a kind face. I thought you'd be kind to me.'

'Did you think of me?'

I admired how he could multitask his tongue for both words and pleasure. I made a mental note to ask him to perform the same trick on me.

'I thought about you a lot. My sister said I thought about you too much.'

Her long nails delicately traced the shape of his earlobe.

'What did you think about?'

'When you visit us on Saturday afternoons, I am terribly nervous all morning. I want to be the one who talks with you, who touches you. I want to be the one.'

Lily lost herself in the moment with David. The girl may have forgotten I was in the room. I'd remind her of her place afterward. He was *my* boyfriend.

'I wondered about you, Lily. You were so quiet.'

'Did you ever think of me?'

Uh oh. How could he possibly answer this question?

'Of course, I thought of you, Lily.'

Good boy. Her hips bucked a little harder at his words.

'Oh? Sometimes I think of you when I have a customer. I close my eyes and imagine it's you instead. It excites me more when I think about telling you any of this. It makes me hot telling you this right now. Is that crazy?'

'No. You're perfectly healthy. You're perfect, Lily.'

My pussy was getting so warm and wet watching him play with her body and her feelings.

'I always wondered what it would feel like to kiss and touch you, David.'

'And now you have me.'

Good job. I smiled.

She fell quiet, then stiff. Her back formed a sudden arch. Her mouth gaped and then a howl escaped her. It was hard to imagine this mousy girl would be one of those lucky ones who have orgasms like rolling thunder. Her feet peddled back and forth like she was trying to reel back from the overwhelming pleasure. However, the rest of her body disagreed and wanted to stay right there forever. David held fast to her pussy. He was determined to ride it out until she was done. Watching her eyes roll back in her head lit a fire beneath my skin.

She finally finished cumming and collapsed among the ruins of her self-control. He decorated her legs with kisses, crawled over her body, and kissed her on the lips. She sat up with a start as if his mouth filled her with a second wind. She couldn't get enough of his lips. I stood from my chair and approached my lovely couple. I pulled David's socks off his feet and helped him out of his pants. They went on the pile. Lily poked a nail at his plump stiff cock and grinned.

'Did I make that?'

'You made that.'

I lifted my dress from Lily's body in a slow reveal and then carefully folded it and placed it back in my cupboard. I watched David's eyes pop at her spectacular nipples. His mouth was on them so fast that Lily seemed whiplashed. I'd seen several customers respond the same way. She should've been used to this reaction, but she was atypically delighted that my David liked them so much. I drew in a sharp breath every time he sucked her firm nips into his mouth. She cradled his head in her hands. He sought salvation in her breasts as if he'd found light in the dark.

They shifted their bodies so they sat and faced one another. Their legs wrapped around the other's body. She placed her left hand on his shoulder and sought his rail-hard cock with her right. Then she made it disappear into her pussy. She fucked my boyfriend in slow deliberate wave-like motions. Her forehead was pressed to his forehead. Each breath she took was a gasp as if he were filling up every empty space inside her. I could tell she was replenishing something that was denied to her. I knelt behind him on my bed and kissed the nape of his neck. I placed my palms upon his back and felt his muscles tense and bunch every time Lily rode up and down his cock. Her nails dug a trail of ten lovely scratches across his shoulder blades. A single nail broke off and lodged deep into his flesh. A blood stain bloomed like a flower on my fresh linen. I marveled at the scene as if it held the beauty and wonder of a sunrise.

I forbade customers to tie up my girls. However, customers were bound as much as they liked. That was my rule at work, but this was a night of play. He retrieved my white silk scarf from inside a pillow while he searched deep in Lily's eyes for the right cue.

She mouthed an enthusiastic *yes*.

His smile turned wicked.

'The safe word is Mao Zedong.'

'I'm familiar with the safe word. It was actually my idea.'

She shot a knowing grin at me.

He tied her hands to the bedhead with my scarf. He knelt between her open thighs and wedged his cock against her vulva so her labia hugged his shaft between her folds. I watched his ass writhe in small circles. I'd wager she was feeling his cock rub her pussy the right way. I reached under the bed and retrieved a wooden bowl of baby oil I stowed there before dinner. This was a blend I double-boiled with virgin coconut oil. I reserved it for my own personal use. He made a cup of his palm and scooped up a serving of the clear viscous liquid. He slowly drizzled it from her belly button to her throat. He then ran his slick hands up and down her slippery tummy and breasts, pinching her nipples along the way. Sometimes he dashed his hands up to her throat where he gave her neck a squeeze. Her mouth yawned open in surprised pleasure whenever he squeezed her windpipe in his fist. He made her whole body a slippery wet mess. Her toes curled in time with his strokes up and down her body.

I could tell by the look in his eyes, he was deciding it was time to fuck her again. He lifted her ass and shoved a pillow underneath it so he could nail her from the most dominant angle (another trick I taught him). He slid his body over hers and laid on top of her. The oil clung to their bodies like a smooth glistening second skin. Now they were both a mess of oil and sweat, and so was my bed. They locked lips and drank from each other's mouths, sharing something intangible beyond my clumsy words. He reached down below and slid his cock deep inside her and held it there, not moving. She squirmed in frustration that he refused to pound her pussy already. She mewled in protest between kisses. He was such a bastard. He then closed both hands over her throat and stared straight into her eyes. His grin was both wickedly awful and awfully wicked. She poked her tongue at him. I'd have been a lot nastier. Then he finally fucked her—hard. He spread her legs so wide it looked as if he was trying to split her apart like a wishbone. If he ever managed to break her apart, I knew exactly what I'd wish for. I remembered her words a moment ago.

You have a kind face. I thought you'd be kind to me.

Her bound hands clenched open and closed against the head of my bed. Her pretty pink nails fluttered like trapped butterflies. I bet he'd never heard her potty mouth until that night.

'Oh, David.

Fuck me.

Fuck me!

Love me.

Fuck me!

David!'

I dug around his overnight bag and found his *Polaroid* camera. I snapped about three ten-packs of instant photographs between bouts of playing with myself. The spent cartridges were tossed in the corner with our growing pile of discarded items. Somewhere in that pile were all of our inhibitions.

I returned to my chair, crossed my legs, and gave a command.

'Come on, David. Fuck her like you mean it!'

He shifted into overdrive and slammed her cunt harder and faster. I knew from years of working with her, she could take all of that punishment and more. Nevertheless, I bet she never felt so wet and welcoming. Her thick hair spilled out like a pool of black blood over the head of my bed. Her little chin pointed directly at the ceiling. A main artery swelled and throbbed in her neck. She was trying to say words, but all she could manage was gibberish. The only thing she could articulate was his name.

Thirty instant *Polaroids* were scattered across the floor of my home. The gaudy images rising to the surface of the film were of a tied-up girl getting fucked into next week by my boyfriend.

I was totally satisfied.

DAVID

I awoke curled up between two women. I had been dreaming of puppies sleeping in a tangle of fur. It was better than the empty space that always trapped me in my sleep. The sun was rising, and Dolly's room gradually filled with light and warmth. My gift was mounted on the wall opposite her bed. I stared at my painting of Dolly as Lin Daiyu. A sparrow chirped outside with some urgency in her throat.

Lily's mouth was pressed into my spine. Her snoring was oddly comforting. The rhythm of her turbulent breathing against my back helped me doze off. I could also feel sticking plaster on my shoulder. She was thoughtful enough to dress my wound before we all kissed goodnight.

My habit was to wake up before Dolly and watch her sleep. I was big-spooning her so that all of me was all over her. I could feel her breathing long and deep like someone who was sleeping soundly perhaps for the first time in a long time. Her lashes rested against her cheeks. Her eyelids twitched from the dreams caught in her eyes. I imagined her as a young girl growing up to become the woman I love.

I counted all the points of contact between our three bodies. There was so much skin between us. We were a mad experiment, an alchemy of mimetic desire. I counted all the prudish values Dolly and I violated over the years. Our love was bold. I was afraid our hubris would catch up to us. I was afraid of how we would pay for our borrowed time.

Six

DAVID

Tiananmen Square or The Gate of Heavenly Peace is one of the largest public spaces in the world, and that is all it is—a large empty space in China's capital. Nothing is there except nothingness. No one thought to plant a tree, a garden, a water feature, or anything that would invite a person to feel a connection. This vast desert of concrete speaks to the insignificance of the individual before the heavy hand of the State.

On June 9th, 1989, Australian Prime Minister, Bob Hawke, read from a classified diplomatic cable during a memorial service for the victims of the Tiananmen Square Massacre.

When all those who had not managed to get away were either dead or wounded, foot soldiers went through the square bayoneting or shooting anybody who was still alive. They had orders that nobody in the square be spared, and children and young girls were slaughtered, anti-personnel carriers and tanks then ran backwards and forwards over the bodies of the slain until they were reduced to pulp, after which, bulldozers moved in to push the remains into piles which were then incinerated by troops with flamethrowers.

Without consulting anyone but his own conscience, the Prime Minister granted permanent visas to 42,000 Chinese people visiting Australia. Eventually they became Australian citizens who built new lives and families.

The sun rising over Tiananmen Square on June 5th, 1989, was not the typical dawn of a bright new day. This was a gray fog gathering some sort of light to reveal the carnage left behind. This was the morning after a massacre of the people in the People's Square.

Nearby along the Street of Eternal Peace, a convoy of army tanks were regrouping after a long night of crushing civil disobedience. Their rattling, gas-guzzling motors spewed noxious white farts of diesel smoke into the already smoggy morning. These were substandard Chinese knockoffs of the standard Soviet *T-54* tank—and they were dancing! Their iron hulls wagged from side to side as if pleased with themselves. Their turrets swiveled obnoxiously. Inside each bloated steel shell were four men made of soft tissue and hardened hearts.

Something happened that nobody expected, let alone the tank crew. There was a young man walking home, a bag of groceries in each hand. He walked in front of the lead tank and stood there. The line of tanks ground to a halt. The man yelled and yelled at whoever was inside. The lead tank turned to go around him. The man walked in front of the tank. The tank turned the other way, and the man stepped in front of it again. They did this a couple of more times until the lead tank turned off its motor. The other tanks followed suit and the silence was deafening. Within minutes of his modest act of defiance, someone took him away. Did he ever find his way home again? Footage captured of this lone dissident was repeated ad infinitum on television screens across the rest of the world. The person who became known as the Tank Man intrigued and moved the world outside of China.

On the other hand, Chinese news banned all footage of this man and the massacre. To this day, the images are blocked in China thanks to an arrangement between the Communist Party and Google. Tank Man was the inconvenient image that cost Beijing the 2000 Olympics.

I saw footage of the Tiananmen Square Massacre for the first time in 2007 at the National Gallery of Victoria, Australia. The grainy video played over and over like a dirty VHS tape stuck on a loop. Every painful memory of the massacre flooded back to me.

The Communist Party purported to be the People's Party. Yet, the people would no longer tolerate their greed and corruption. Criminals were officiated, and in turn, officials were criminalized. There were uprisings in hundreds of cities across China. Scattered embers were fanned into one fire.

One of the most organized protests was in our city of Chengdu. I was barely aware of the fuss as I was too preoccupied with learning a duet with Dolly. We planned to sing our song at the *Shangri-La Bar*. Every year we returned to sing together in their annual karaoke competition. People remembered us, and we even had a modest following. It was frivolous in hindsight. The world would never forget the protests happening at the time. Meanwhile, I was walking down the street blocking out the noise, listening to my new Sony *Discman*.

When I arrived at her parlor, I found the doors locked. An icicle of fear crystallized inside me. The locked door felt ominous. The few people left on the street were all walking hastily in one direction. Some were wearing white bandanas of white or red. I took off my headphones and walked with them.

After a couple of hours, we reached a sea of protesters at Chunxi Road. Hundreds of thousands converged upon this rally point. It was part carnival, part street rally. They paraded on foot and on bicycles, beating drums, and chanting slogans from small squeaky bull horns. Some were singing the *Internationale* song.

We are nothing, let us be everything.

There were teachers, shopkeepers, doctors, nurses, scientists, and members of the army demonstrating. Even Chinese naval officers marched. There were the very old and the very young. There were people in samlors, rickshaws, trucks and buses, and construction vehicles. Bobcats and harvesters served as blockades. All were out there with their complaints written large on placards built with bamboo frames. There was only one demographic not represented, the Communist Party who caused all of this resentment.

There was a common look fixed on the faces of the protesters. It was a look outside of my lived experience. The general oppression rarely touched me. A *gweilo* like me would never know what it felt like to be locked inside an invisible prison.

It looked like the old regime was about to fall. Indeed, it was hard to imagine how any other scenario would be possible. Surely, when faced with these numbers, cooler heads would prevail?

The Party elders feared the whole edifice of communism was going to collapse. They had seen it collapse in the Soviet Union and other parts of Eastern Europe. They needed to save face and cow their population back into submission. Supreme Party Leader Deng Xiaoping sent orders to quell the protests by force.

The first rounds of bullets caught everyone by surprise. The people in the streets did not expect this to happen.

The police shot randomly in all directions.

A young man standing next to me shouted, "Anti-fascism!" The police then shot at us.

Two people in front of me were cut down by gunfire.

We threw ourselves to the ground. People behind me were falling. The police shot everybody, including doctors, nurses, and rescuers. They spared no one.

The entire time I felt a panic rising inside of me that I must find Dolly. I needed to be sure she was safe. I closed my eyes and imagined where she would most likely be during a time like this.

Our rooftop.

I got to my feet and looked for a way out of there.

The tear-gassing began in earnest. Soon many people were donning disposable medical masks. I lifted my shirt collar over my mouth and nose, kept my head down, and sprinted toward a laneway between two shops.

Eventually, after a few wrong turns, I found the old Department of Finance building. The door was ajar and held open by a brick. I dashed inside and toward the elevator. I repeatedly hit the UP button like everyone else does with the insane idea this will make it go faster. It took forever to arrive and another forever to spill me out onto the rooftop.

I found Dolly. She was helping several people assemble a banner large enough to be seen from both the street and the sky. In both Mandarin and English, it read, "Of the people, by the people, for the people." She wore her black poly-cotton slacks, a bone white silk blouse and a white bandana bearing words that demanded nothing less than democracy.

I ran into her arms—pathetically happy to find her safe. She embraced me in kind, covering my face with kisses while whispering the words, 'Sorry, *qīnài de*. Sorry, I couldn't let you know about my plans today, but I'm glad you found me.'

Her friends looked bewildered by the unexpected appearance of this Western-looking youth. A couple of them wore white bandanas as well. One wore a T-shirt emblazoned with the word, 自由 (liberty) in red paint. Something important was happening.

I volunteered to help them install their banner. We rushed out of there as soon as the job was finished.

Not long after our group hit the street, a man was shot down a block away. Someone ran up and dragged the man to cover. We kept running. On my left side, someone was hit in the neck. Right in front of us, a tall man, about forty-years-old, fell to the ground. He was shot in the chest. Blood was pouring from a hole in his body. We were as shocked as he was. We had no idea how to stop the bleeding. Someone found a bicycle to carry him in the direction of the hospital.

Two people were lifting another injured person by their arms and running away from the gunfire. Some were carried away on a makeshift litter made of bamboo and blankets.

A doctor was performing mouth-to-mouth resuscitation, her face stained with blood.

An ambulance appeared to attend to those who were on the ground. The police opened fire again until black smoke blew from the ambulance radiator. It smashed into a clothes shop window. The driver slumped over the wheel.

The outfits worn by the Chinese police in the 1980s were almost interchangeable with the army uniforms in design. The eerie similarity was not lost on me. The police marched through the litter of broken placards, abandoned bicycles, and fallen bodies.

By then we lost the other members of our group. Only Dolly and I remained. She found a narrow alley, grabbed my hand, and we made our escape from the chaos. We dashed through a maze of laneways. The further we ran from Chunxi Road, the more relieved I felt we were a safe distance from harm.

We spilled out onto a main street that appeared empty at first, except when we looked on either side and found both sides blocked. The protesters were on one end and the police blocked the other. Each side seemed to be waiting for the other to fire the first bullet or throw the first rock. The tension broke and the air exploded with gunfire.

Dolly was hit by a stray bullet. She collapsed onto the ground. Her body splayed across the road among the rubbish and the blood. I fell to her side and lay beside her. Comforting words fell hopelessly out of my mouth as blood pooled around her leg. Thick dark red life was leaving her. Her face was drained of its color.

I felt two sets of hands trying to haul me away from her. She and I held onto each other while another policeman tried to pry her from my grip. She let out such a baleful scream it broke my heart in two. Her blouse tore open, exposing her to further humiliation.

'Stop! Please!' I screamed. I may as well have screamed into a monsoon. The police were brutal. Their batons swung without mercy at both our bodies. Their blunt words were as clipped and loud as machine gunfire. They called us disgusting things. One of the policemen laughed. Another slammed his bloodied baton across Dolly's arm hard enough for her to let go of me. There was the sound of breaking bone followed by her scream that ran through me like a razorblade.

She was taken away into the gaping maw of a police van.

Terror works. There was a method to the madness of overwhelming force—to shock, terrify, and awe. Chinese television portrayed the protesters as counter-revolutionaries, hooligans, and Western agents. No one knows for certain how many people died or disappeared. In the aftermath of the massacre, tens of thousands were arrested all across the country. Some are still in prison today. Have you ever seen a Chinese policeman manhandle a citizen? They are brutal. They twist your arm. They bend you over. They punch you a few times. They kick you. Did the police do this to Dolly? Did they bend her beautiful body as they shuttled her from one prison to another?

The Party executed unknown numbers of civilians. Many public executions were broadcast on CCTV shortly afterward. Was Dolly among the dead?

As I have mentioned, a *gweilo* like me would never know how it feels to live every waking moment subjugated. I suffered some bruises, cuts, and a concussion during the protest. However, because of what I am, I was neither imprisoned nor disappeared.

The police let me go, but my heart was still under arrest. They would not tell me where Dolly was taken. A missing loved one causes a different kind of grief than death. There is no funeral for your loss.

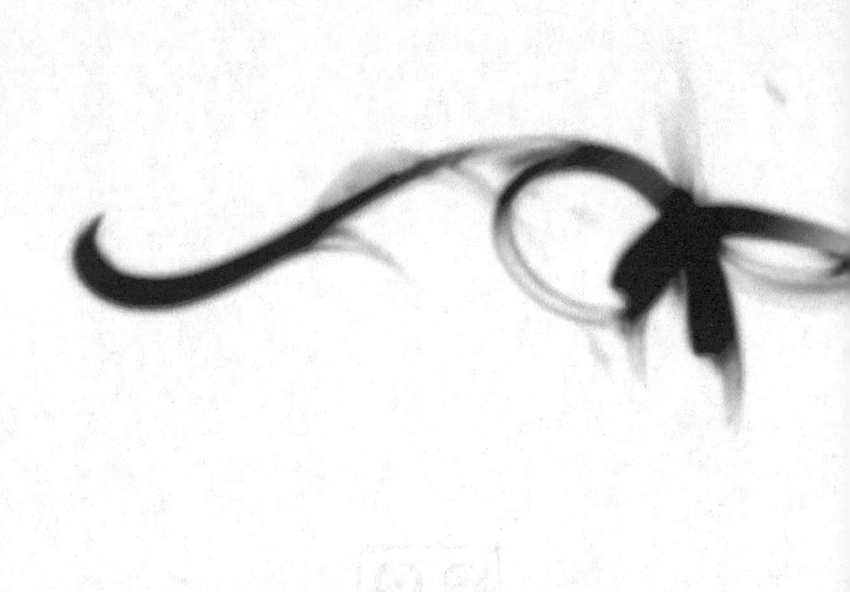

Seven

Dolly was not alone among the disappeared. Lily and Cici were gone as well. I hoped they fled China like Mei Mei. I found her keys to our apartment on my bed with a sweet note written in careful, child-like English.

I see in your eyes how much you care.
You will always be my endless love.

She broke her promise that she would never leave me. Twenty-years later, she reached out to me from Canada. She used a digital meeting place called Facebook. It was banned in China, but promised to connect the world. Her profile photo led me to believe she had not aged a day, but that may have been the result of clever filters. She married again. This man stayed home.

Many people were suddenly absent. They vanished like the man who stood in front of the tank with his grocery bags, only to be rushed off the stage.

A Faustian deal was struck between the Party and the people. In the wake of Tiananmen, the Party opened the economy to the people to create a comfortable middle class. No more struggling to hold their head above water. The opportunity for wealth was there for the taking on one condition: do not bite the hand that feeds. The Party had demonstrated what would happen to demonstrators. An era of civil obedience followed thereafter.

The massacre drew a bloody line in the country's history. There was the old communist China and a new one that sought to seduce foreign investors. The Party carved out *special economic zones*. These were exclusive places free to invite foreign money. The country welcomed hundreds of billions of foreign dollars every year. China shifted into economic overdrive. Paddy fields were replaced by concrete jungles. China's rise as an economic behemoth was the story of the 21st century. It all began after the smoke cleared from the massacre.

Never in the course of human history had such a large number of people gathered more wealth in such a short time. There were 200 million middle-class Chinese that did not heretofore exist. The terrible genius was the art of buying off unhappiness.

No dream seemed impossible, and no expense too daunting or pointless. The high-speed train line from Shanghai airport used technology too expensive for its German engineers. China made it possible, even if the train was often empty. The Party indulged in delusions of cultural grandeur. They built art galleries, libraries, museums, and opera houses that nobody asked for. The joke was that China no longer inspired free artistic expression. As a result, the libraries were too censored to bother perusing. The museums preserved only lies. Some opera houses did not even have opera singers.

Underpinning this extravagant spending, almost all Western production migrated from the West to China. The country became a factory for the world. Now it was in everyone's best interest to be friends with China. Tank Man vanished from Western television screens. The massacre became a footnote. It was reduced to a local complaint that dare not interfere with the obscene amount of money at stake. The Party had performed a clever sleight of hand in international relations.

As I stood there in the rubble, smoke, and blood on that day, I would never have imagined the same deep vein of corruption and thuggery would remain unchecked. The same Party elites who ordered the mass murder would remain enthroned. I would never have imagined that one day one of them would declare himself dictator for life.

I buried myself in my ambition to dull the pain. I figured this would be more productive and less clichéd than turning to alcohol. Ambition bites the nails of success and I bit until I bled. In time, I became an aggressively enterprising design prodigy in the New China. Dressed in my father's Armani suits, I made my bones pressing the flesh with everyone who was able to help me up the ladder. As Japan's star waned, China's red star rose, and I rose with it.

I changed the way I spoke so people would like me more. My awkward geek-tech talk was replaced by charming, but empty, platitudes. Years of listening to Chinese academics bullshit me and my classmates helped me refine the art of sounding wise while not saying anything at all. Years of watching Dolly taught me to evoke a pleasant nothingness that pleased everybody and threatened nobody. I spent the 1990s smiling until my face hurt. I practiced in the mirror, making sure it appeared authentic. I shoved my awful glasses under my desk and switched to contact lenses. They were tinted to make my eyes appear a brighter green. Nevertheless, these changes did not feel like enough. I needed something more dramatic to reinvent myself for the new era. The solution was a haircut.

I took a trip to South Korea to represent a Chinese design firm whose name was as forgettable as their work. Nevertheless, they held political clout I wished to borrow. I pretended I was every cosmopolitan myth they projected onto me. The company had no idea I had not set foot outside of China. I was one of a selection of delegates from all over the world who were invited to Seoul to discuss building a space for two of Rodin's most colossal sculptures. While standing in front of Rodin's *The Gates of Hell*, it occurred to me why I was eager to make the trip. The artist sculpted a maelstrom of suffering, forbidden love, punishment, unabashed sexuality, maternal love, and I remembered. Dolly loved Rodin.

I scheduled a spare day to roam the colorful Yongsan district. There was a buoyant feeling everywhere I looked. All those charming shops, narrow cobbled alleys, and lush parks were built by people light of heart. South Koreans seemed to stand straighter and live with less fear than the people in my country. It was a thread that ran through everything they touched.

Perhaps this is the reason why South Korean hairdressers were ahead of the style game. I walked into the most chic salon in the neighborhood with a copy of the November '96 *Rolling Stone* magazine in my hand. I showed the stylist a page from the magazine. She let out a muted squeal of excitement. My long hair was hacked off. It lay in a pile at my feet. Mei Mei would have screamed if she witnessed such blasphemy. The stylist recreated a near-perfect impression of the side-curtain hairstyle worn by Leonardo DiCaprio in Baz Luhrman's film, *Romeo + Juliet*. The reinvention was complete.

The company booked me a ticket to Taipei the following day. I was to make nice with a marketing rep from one of Taiwan's incredible microchip manufacturers. Democracy had earned Taiwanese supremacy in silicon that China could not match without stealing their ideas. That was why I was not allowed in their labs. However, I was happy to discover there was a delicious Szechuan hot pot dinner to honor their guest.

Rather than take a cab back to my hotel room, I walked the streets of the capital. Lose yourself in any city for an hour and you will eventually find yourself reflected in its surfaces. The best cities are halls of mirrors.

It was surreal to be surrounded by people who looked Chinese, but they were not. There was an ease in their expression to which I was not accustomed. They spoke the same language, but there was a sleek curve to their Mandarin accent. Taiwan is a thriving, peaceful, happy nation. It is what China could have been. If only Mao had not taken the whole country on a communist detour on the way to falling in love with what it claimed to oppose—capitalism.

I was melancholy. The air was still fragrant with the scent of rain from the thunderstorm that afternoon. The wet streets reflected back the city's neon lights and a flash of leftover lightning.

Then I saw her from behind.

In the fingertips of her right hand, she held a tall cup of iced tea. It swung absently by her side as she walked ahead of me. Her clothes were different and yet the same. She wore a fashionably '90s black satin slip dress. Her hair was piled up in a carefully careless updo drawing my eye to where the slim straps met her shoulders. Dolly would never have felt free enough to bare her defined shoulders in China. This is what she may have worn if fate found her in a more liberal country where a woman was free to wear underwear as outerwear. Underneath the lush fabric, her body moved in a familiar feline gait. She was filled with purpose, but she was not in a hurry to get there.

I followed her far enough away so she would not catch my reflection in the store windows. But I stayed close enough so I may scan for any hint she was indeed my Dolly. Every time she paused to cross the road, she raised her cup to her mouth and drew a sip from a thick straw. She was enjoying her freedom as if it were a light breeze on her face. There was not a trace of fear. Her lips wore a familiar curl, or was it a trick my mind played on me?

The lightning struck a second time and lit up her profile. She was not Dolly, but a wraith meant to haunt me. A question was stuck in my mouth.

Are we so enamored with beauty that we would gladly allow a ghost to haunt us so long as it were beautiful?

The stranger stopped outside *The Hilton*. She drained the last of the tea, tossed the cup into a trash bin, and disappeared through the hotel's grandiose revolving door. I fished out the cup from the bin, not caring how shameless I looked to passers-by. The cup smelled of basic green tea, not peach oolong.

She was just a wish.

Was her memory all that was left for me now?

When I returned to China's capital, my first meeting involved stealing a State contract out of the mouth of a competitor. The task was designing yet another heroic monument to Zhou Enlai, one of several lionized founders of the People's Republic. The job was an easy bit of overripe nationalist nonsense, but it was obscenely profitable.

I pressed fifty-three on the elevator keypad. The cabin was one of those units lined floor to ceiling with mirrors. The occupant is meant to feel less claustrophobic. I checked my look in the mirror. I changed my clothes, my hair, and my face. My father's elegant navy Armani suit complimented my nonchalant new hairstyle. I saw in my eyes and the set in my jaw the things everyone else would see: composure, confidence, and charisma. I never let anyone get close enough to discover what was missing—happiness.

I found myself in a typical boardroom designed for the New China. Business environments built after the massacre were Chinese knockoffs of the office spaces seen in the film, *Wall Street*. The film's credo, "greed is good", was not meant to be taken literally. Like many great stories from the West, the fable was lost in translation.

The woman presiding over the meeting was composed of sharp angles of expensive fabric and self-importance. She leaned toward me.

'What's the name of your cologne? It reminds me of the sea breeze on a beach I want to visit.'

'*Acqua di Gio* by Armani... to go with the suit.'

'New?'

'My suit or the scent?

She giggled with an unexpected girlishness.

'The scent.'

'No. It hasn't been released in China yet. I've a friend who helps me find these things.'

'Friends are important.'

She was doing that thing Chinese women do to signal they are interested in fucking you. It is subtle. If you blink you will miss it. I held her gaze for a moment longer than I should. She fiddled with her papers and knocked her thousand-dollar *Mont Blanc* pen off the table. An assistant scurried over and retrieved it for her. Men with jade eyes make Chinese women forget themselves. The married executive was one of the most powerful members of the Communist Party.

I discovered how numb you have to be to touch someone intimately without even the slightest chemistry to coax you along. None of these influential women who visited me were good looking. They came and went from my studio apartment in a bashful rush or an inexplicable swagger. Occasionally I would sketch their comical demeanor in my art journals. This is how I dealt with my peculiar situation.

I took a great leap of faith in myself and opened my own design house, *Gossamer*. It was a Chinese simulacrum of British design studios like *Wolf Ollins* and *Pentagram* born out of the 1960s and '70s. The English define gossamer as fine spider silk. However, the Chinese read gossamer as the balance spring in a timepiece. Without this fine steel spiral, the clock loses time. I enjoyed the ambiguity in my brand name. My portfolio included a cross-disciplinary range of architectural, fashion, public space, and fine arts projects. Would my father have been proud of me if he were still alive?

He died in his Upper West Side apartment in Manhattan before the new millennium. At the funeral, wife number-seven told me he died in her arms. I discovered he started new families in several cities across the globe, as if he were a franchise. I was introduced to a mess of half-siblings at the funeral. I looked into his open casket and found nothing I recognised.

Fashion houses collaborated with me on everything from wedding dresses to obscenely over-priced designer backpacks. I was interviewed on every stupid TV show to great applause. Idiots from equally idiotic talk shows asked me who I was dating? When will I find a wife? I smiled and feigned a bashful demeanor. The whole country was enamored with this homegrown successful *gweilo* speaking perfect Chinese. My name and brand came to represent the dream of modern China and its competitive posturing with the West. My image was both a cross-cultural commodity and a fetishised oddity. I allowed the media to dress me like an expensive *yáng wá wa* (Caucasian doll).

I drove around in the understated luxury of a 1999 Audi *S8*. I discovered the car in an action film called *Ronin*. I bought one for me, painted Ebony Pearl, and another in Casablanca White For Dolly, in case I ever found her. Hope is a bitch. On the tape deck I played a well-worn cassette from my Walkman days. A track from 1984 was on repeat. The singer's voice was an effortless quiet storm cool. Her song described a lover boy living a diamond life under city lights and business nights. No place for the sensitive heart. Not a place to end but somewhere to start.

I lived above a cavernous workshop sponsored by the State. The space was filled with the sharp smell of paints, thinners, wood shavings, plaster, clay, splattered easels, brushes clogged with gouache, *Itoya* pencils sharpened down to their stubs, and too many books filled with the drawings of Egon Schiele and Da Vinci. On any day of the week, my shop was packed with modest commission pieces I sold for immodest prices, colossal State projects, and a select number of worker bees who helped with the big jobs.

One of those bees was Jolin. She made all my frames and managed my events. However, her collaboration with me paled in comparison to her stellar career in curating art galleries. She had her work cut out for her. There were far too many galleries in China for a country whose artistic expression was tethered to "national pride".

Her wardrobe profited from her success. My oldest friend was no longer the moderate wallflower I met in school. She often dressed in chic loose turtlenecks and smart tapered pants. She preferred solid dramatic colors. Her most striking fashion statement was her modish hairstyle. She wore a controlled updo with a side-sweep. Her signature scent was Thierry Mugler's *Angel*—an indulgent bittersweetness that followed her everywhere.

We spent many afternoons enjoying tea and good company in my Balinese pergola. I built it outside my workshop near where the Fuhe River flowed. There was a view of a masonry bridge built a thousand years ago. I never got around to crossing that bridge.

'David, I don't know how you can stomach that vile ginseng tea.'

'It's good for my love life.'

'Yeah, I've heard about that.'

'How's your love life?'

She let a coy chuckle escape between sips of jasmine tea.

'There *is* one man.'

'Do I know him?'

'You know *of* him, but you don't know him.'

I was intrigued.

'Why are you not with him now? You seem to spend a lot of your time at my workshop.'

That coy chuckle again.

'He seems preoccupied with another.'

'I'm sure he's missing out on the better of the two girls.'

'She can't love him, it's true—not like I do.'

'Does he know this?'

'A long time ago, I thought he saw me once—actually *saw* me. I've been holding on to that moment all these years, waiting for him to *see* me again. You know what? I haven't said this out loud before. Now that I have, I hear how foolish I sound. I think it's time I closed that chapter.'

Then she recited the lyrics of *Madama Butterfly* in perfect Italian.

'E aspetto, e aspetto gran tempo.'
(And I wait, and I wait for a long time)

This was the aria in my head when we kissed in the rain a lifetime ago. How could she have known? She turned her face toward the river and wiped something from her eye.

'He's not worth your tears, Jolin, and the one who's worth it, won't make you cry.'

Every detail of my apartment was staged like a display home selling a lifestyle that's never been lived outside a catalog. The space was curated to weather the scrutiny of visiting customers and lovers. More often than not they were both things in the same person. They would nod approvingly at my nouveau riche dump, confirming my suspicion that I should seek better company than theirs. I hated every elitist book of German philosophy on the shelf, every stick of Scandi furniture, every vapid vase and hollow sculpture. On the other hand, I finally had a big living room window that opened, but I missed the view of the tai chi ladies from home. The people outside my new window shuffled in corporate clothes to corporate jobs. The New Chengdu grew another skyscraper every month, so I no longer saw the sun set over the horizon. Instead, it made a quiet retreat behind cranes and concrete.

My mother's photo album lay on the nook of the window. It had not been opened since her funeral. When I took it from the packing box and placed it under my window, I was careful not to consider it too much. I had every intention to crack it open one lazy afternoon, but I always found some other distraction on a lazy afternoon.

Her album lay there like a sleeping snake. It was custom made, covered in white satin brocade, an anniversary gift from my father. There were exactly 120 photographs of her, one for every month they were married.

I knocked it open one day. I was rushing around, turning the place upside down trying to find my MicroTAC flip phone that was ringing from somewhere in my apartment. The cell phone trilled and trilled until the caller gave up and the thing fell silent. I'd made a mess. Pillows were strewn. Magazines were scattered. The photo album lay on the floor. Photographs of my mother were spilled onto the carpet.

It was not her familiar image that made my eyes hurt. Rather, it was a photo of the unfamiliar that broke me. A small note penciled below the 5x7 print read, age *23*. She was my age, sitting high on a rock wet with sea spray. Her face was softer. Her hair cut short like a boy, like I had never seen before. She wore a man's white button-down shirt. Could it have been my father's? I never saw her wear anything else but dresses. She stared at the waves on a black and white beach I will never know. The story of how she came to be there, I will never hear. The photograph was taken a long time before I was a thought that even crossed her mind. It was a moment frozen in time before she needed to make any important decisions about anything, like marrying the man who took the picture. I needed my father beside me to explain. I needed my dad.

There was little chance another copy was made, and no chance of finding the negative from which it was printed. It was a precious artifact made from photosensitive grains of silver and halides on Kodak paper. The photograph was the strongest evidence that my mother was nothing so reductive as a mother. Her name was Josephine and she was a person whose life was as prone to pain and as pregnant with possibility as my own. Her slender body was balanced on a rock. Her knees were drawn to her chest. Twelve years later she died wearing a hospital gown and a plastic tube down her throat. She took her last breath alone, while my father was in the emergency room paying the bill.

I always assumed I may one day shed a quiet tear flipping through her photographs. It was meant to be dignified. I never expected to collapse in a bawling mess on my floor where her album lay open like an unanswered question.

It took three months of bribes and bureaucracy to find the Beijing hospital where she died. I made an appointment. The following Wednesday I sat waiting in an office chair opposite the administrator. He was busy on the telephone trying to figure out what to do with several baby girls abandoned in the maternity ward. The man used his free hand to compulsively click his pen. The nervous staccato matched the tightly wound tension in his voice. It occurred to me that uncovering technical details about my mother's death would not make her any less dead. I walked out before the administrator could finish solving the problem of the orphaned girls.

I wrote a letter to my mother, slipped it behind the last page of her album and returned it to the window nook. It was a mercy that none of my visitors were intellectually curious enough to open it. Memories of Josephine were left to rest in peace.

Ever since the massacre, I paid for lessons every Wednesday afternoon at the Go Chess school underneath Dolly's old flat. I discovered the Master's name was Li-Jie. In a previous life he traveled back and forth between Beijing and Tokyo playing long, silent matches against his opposite numbers in Japan. The Master remembered Dolly with the goodness of a doting uncle. He knew why I was there. I stole an occasional glance toward the stairs and imagined her standing at the foot of the stairwell. He recognised the burnt out lightbulbs in my eyes.

My greatest lesson had nothing to do with Go. One night we were playing our game and the air was thick with silence. No truck nor scooter upset the quiet. We took turns snapping our stones into place on the thick board carved from the trunk of a Kaya tree. The lonely click of our stones in the still night was a calm island in the rough sea of my mind. The words he spoke were the compass I needed.

'It's cloudy tonight, yes?'

'It's been like this for a while.'

'Watch and wait.'

'It's been too long. I miss the moon.'

He stopped halfway to place his white stone among my black stones. I caught his unblinking eye.

'Watch and wait. The clouds will part, and you'll have your moon. *Yuánfèn* (fate) will bring her back to you. Although she may be a thousand miles away.'

He clacked one stone into place and blocked my capture of the rest of his stones. Li-Jie stood up, walked to a cupboard, reached into its highest, deepest recess, and withdrew the most well-worn travel case I have ever laid my eyes on. He handed it to me. I cracked it open and discovered it was crammed with notebooks of every size and color.

'These are the diaries she left behind. Her memories belong to you now.'

I read her diaries deep into the early morning. Some were damaged by mildew and silverfish. I later asked an archivist to restore these diaries so I could read them. The passage which broke my heart was written in a diary disguised as Mao Zedong's *Little Red Book*. Her Mandarin characters were jagged and frantic.

I write these things to taste my bitterness twice. I was small when the food ran out in China. A famine doesn't only starve you of food. Something else is stripped from you. There's a hole in my belly that can't be filled by food anymore. The knife twist came after the famine. We city students were blamed for the whole thing. All the smart city children were packed onto buses and exiled to the countryside. I was told I was too educated, and my thinking made me decadent. They took my books away so I dare not think again. No longer was I an individual person. I was told to submit myself to the collective. I felt no different than the livestock we were made to tend. Our clothes were so drab and shapeless we even looked like cows, for fucks' sake! I felt sick to my stomach when I remembered those ugly blue and green outfits and that stupid cap. There were crackdowns against the anti-revolutionaries—whatever that means. It was a slaughter, and we were the lambs. I'm lucky to have escaped back to the city, but I felt bad for those I left behind. What's so special about me that I survived?

I was both sad and glad to understand the things that shaped the woman I loved. Why did she not tell me this? I wonder if she felt I was too young or privileged to understand. My admiration for her only deepened in her absence. I wanted to be the hero she needed me to be. I wanted to hold her and reassure her no one would ever hurt her again. I wept because she was not with me to hold.

Among the diaries was a hard envelope secured with twine. Inside was a page torn from my old art journal sandwiched carefully between layers of tissue paper. It was my first drawing of her straddling the window ledge. Her eyes were somewhere between beauty and play. She was bathed in the afternoon sun a million years ago. My heart broke a little more.

I was on the floor of my ridiculous apartment. I spread her diaries all around me trying to find a way to reach her. I was surrounded by the broken parts of the one I love.

A tea cup is more beautiful after it has been broken and lovingly pieced back together. I was reading about a Japanese aesthetic called *wabi sabi*. It proposes that the details of beauty are in its delicate imperfections, the reminders that it survived and was loved enough to be held again. To hold her again...

I often worked until midnight on a project I dared not tell another Chinese soul. I permanently borrowed the *Rand* tablet from my old university. During the day, this museum piece sat under a dust cover against the largest of my workshop windows. After dark, anyone passing by may catch a man afflicted by a fever-dream of creativity. I was re-imagining this 1964 relic into something that would forever change lives, especially mine.

The *Rand* was only 10 x 10 inches. With a resolution of 100 lines per inch. I upsized it to a far more useful 10 x 20 inches and 5000 LPI. I experimented with different plastics and fabrics so the tablet surface felt textured like paper. I did not like that the stylus was attached to the tablet by a wire. I thought a wireless version would liberate the artist. The stylus itself should look and feel like one of my *Itoya* pencils from Japan.

I collaborated on the down-low with some Japanese engineers referred to me by my father. The pencil they built for me was powered by touching it to the tablet. By the very action of using the pencil, it received power by electronic magnetic resonance. Without batteries, the pencil was as light as one of my *Itoya* pencils.

My pencil boasted thousands of levels of pressure sensitivity and my tablet felt not only the angle of the pencil's tilt, but the artist's demeanor. The pencil would sense if you were rushed and haphazard or slow and deliberate. All of this fuzzy human input was translated onto the computer screen.

After many detailed letters and faxes back and forth, they guided me toward a working prototype of the tablet. I built one version of the tablet on my end according to what I needed as an artist. My Japanese colleagues built a mirror equivalent in their laboratory. Our product, launched in 2004, was named *Wabi-Sabi*. It. It made us a lot of money. I funneled my share to a bank account in Melbourne, Australia. No one in China knew about my covert project until years later. By the time they discovered what I was doing, it was too late. The tablet project was a means to an even more covert end. Not even my Japanese friends knew the greatest design on my easel was a plan to rescue Dolly.

2008 was the year of the Beijing Olympics. I felt a silent disgust for the IOC in allowing a government of thugs to host an event that purports to build a peaceful and better world. Nevertheless, I maneuvered my brand name into the design committee. My company played a pivotal role in the art direction for this absurd pantomime on the international stage. I held my nose and shook the hand of President Hu Jintao.

I was enjoying a level of access most Chinese people could not begin to comprehend. There were few corridors of power left where I had not made friends and allies. One night, I found myself nursing a seriously drunk and seriously powerful member of the Central Committee of the Communist Party. Chinese drinkers insist on imbibing spirits as potent as jet fuel—an unwise choice for people who are prone to a nasty toxic flush reaction from alcohol. The woman was drinking *Kweichow Moutai* all night (The liquor is about 54% alcohol. *Jim Beam* is only 37%). The one thing stopping her from falling was my arm. She was happy to hold onto me. After all, she was obscenely liberal with her hands ever since the day we met during a built environment conference.

We were both lounging in a V.I.P booth in some gaudy nightmare of a Beijing nightclub. The music was one of those terrible fucking tracks from T-Pain or Chris Brown, or worse, a collab of both. Eventually, she became pliable enough to help me with something I was working toward for almost two decades. Across the table, I slid a piece of paper with Dolly's real name, date of birth, and one of my *Polaroid* photographs of her—a close up, her eyes held happiness a hundred years ago. A couple of days later, the Party member provided me with a location.

Eight

China was one of the last places on earth to be spared both the agony and the ecstasy of owning a car. Chinese people suffered a steep learning curve to catch up to the rest of the world of motoring. There were statutory road rules in China, but nobody followed them. To their credit, Chinese people developed exceptional skills in defensive driving. This was necessary as they had to combat an exceptional amount of offensive driving. When accidents happened, the carnage was horrific. Seatbelts were ignored and their warning lights and buzzers were bypassed. Crash helmets were dismissed by motorcyclists. Their wives rode pillion with their babies sandwiched between the parents. So it was with great trepidation that I took a road trip to the country.

I replaced my Audi *S8* saloon with an *R8 Type 42*. The sports car was painted Phantom Black Pearl. I paid extra for the Oxygen Silver side-blades. It was the first *R8* to be driven in China and it was the last time I would drive it.

A seriously ugly accident stopped traffic during my trip. The highway was transformed into a car park of hundreds of gridlocked vehicles. The pile-up was caused by a truck carrying a tree twice as long as the trailer upon which it was roughly strapped. Everyone waited for hours as the shell-shocked and grieving survivors stood around wondering what to do. Accidents were so common that cottage industries popped up in response. Hawkers wandered from car to car selling soup, tea, and water to bored, tired, and parched travelers. The prices were so high they may as well be robbing them. A kid wandered out to the roadside with a chair and a sign written in blunt characters.

Use my toilet. 5 RMB per person.

He sat in his chair and collected cash from desperate people with bladders full of soup, tea, and water. The satisfied smirk on his face embodied the New China—pure opportunistic capitalism thriving in a "communist" economy.

To complicate matters, there seemed to be some confusion about what a road is used for. Corn farmers dried their cobs on the road. Drivers found themselves swerving to dodge their produce. More than once I was saved by the Audi's all-wheel-drive traction. The farmers yelled at me when I drove near their corn. Their sunburnt faces scowled, indignant that I had the gall to use the road for its intended purpose. Some farmers barricaded their corn with broken bottles to flatten your tires. I witnessed a car or two careen off the road and plow into those deathtrap gutters.

There was no roadside assistance. If your car broke down, a local farmer would charge you twice its value to tow it to his cousin's workshop. By workshop, I mean the driveway of his house. Said cousin will charge whatever he likes to fix it. You may as well leave your dead car on the roadside for the scavengers. Welcome to the New China, where hustlers did anything for a seat at the table with the rising middle class.

The worst thing you could do was stop on the roadside for refreshment. There were pirates who waited for idle tourists. Regrettably, this was exactly what I did at the edge of a field of silvergrass.

On a patch of dirt off the bitumen, I found a snack cart with a hand-drawn sign for tanghulu. These were the skewered hawthorn fruits Dolly and I enjoyed along the Funan River. I bought one for myself and one for Dolly. The vendor was a rake-thin man. A flip-phone seemed to be permanently stuck to his ear. He smiled and flashed a gold tooth at me as he took my money.

As I walked back to my car, I remembered the childish joy that spread across Dolly's face whenever we found her favorite snack. The moment I bit into the fruit, five men surrounded my car. They circled and ogled as if they had found a naked woman rather than an assemblage of metal and plastic. I was in trouble.

The tanghulu guy was nowhere to be seen. He probably tipped them off. There would be a handsome referral fee waiting for him. His tanghulu was shit anyway. He was too lazy to take the seeds out of the fruit. I tossed both skewers over my shoulder.

All four men wore fake *Calvin Klein* or *Ralph Lauren* shirts. The oldest and ugliest member appeared to be the spokesperson. His posture arched like a mantis. His hair slicked back with sweat. The others shared his features and could have been his sons and nephews. One of them hawked up phlegm and spat it on the ground in front of me. It didn't impress me. I saw this charming habit every five minutes from men on the streets in the city. The older guy demanded the keys to my car. Violence was implied by iron pipes held behind backs.

I was sure none of them had ever seen a car like this, nor would they ever see one again. I had an idea. I told him it was not enough to simply hand my keys over to him. I convinced him I needed to get in my car and unlock the "special security code" in the steering wheel so he could drive it. I was willing to bet my life they had no idea I was bullshitting. I was surprised they let me climb carefully into the driver's seat. Perhaps they were distracted by the perfect mandarin from the mouth of a gweilo.

The older guy held the door open with one hand whilst brandishing his bent pipe. One of them tried to get into the passenger seat beside me but couldn't figure out how to use the clever flush-line door handle of the R8. An image flickered across the back of my retinas of Dolly dragged into a police van, her bones broken. I took a breath and let it go—long and deep.

I shot my hand out and tried to yank the door from the older guy's grip. He smashed his pipe down onto my fist. The searing pain took me back to the massacre. The memory filled me with the strength to haul the door shut.

I hit the red ignition button on the steering wheel. I slammed the car into gear and floored the accelerator, whipping up a whirlwind of dirt and gravel flying into their stupefied faces. I shut down Safety Mode and punched in Sports Option, shoving all the car's power to the back axle. I spun the steering wheel from left to right and back again, carving a crazy eight-shaped pattern in the earth. A cyclone of debris blasted the gang of four and the abandoned tanghulu stall.

You may ask, where were the police? During the entire road trip, I saw a total of one police car. The blue and white patrol was driven by an off-duty policeman on vacation with relatives.

The pirates must have felt protected by the lawlessness of that remote part of the country. However, it was the same lawlessness that protected me as I chased their leader across a paddock until he dove headfirst into a smelly mangrove swamp. I made a stop at a service station, bandaged my hand, fuelled up, and hit the road again.

After an eight-hour drive, I arrived worse for wear to meet the Chief Warden of a "re-education" prison farm. He was a pirate of a different kind of rape and pillage. His office smelled of corruption and feet. There was an American titty calendar on the wall from 1979. As soon as I sat at his desk, there was a distant scream from somewhere deep inside his prison. I flinched. The Warden did not flinch.

I discovered the State bought and sold Dolly across various labour camps over the many years since her arrest. This prison made sweatshirts for *Tommy Hilfiger*. Considering the labour was of the slave variety, the prison turned a handsome profit for all the Party members involved. I was able to bribe the Warden to release her because she was not a high-value political prisoner. She was considered a nobody. I gave the Warden the keys to my *R8* for his eighteen-year-old kid. The car was worth a quarter-of-a-million US dollars. In exchange, he gave me keys to a 1986 Volkswagen *Santana* station wagon so that I could drive home.

The smug bastard wore such a punchable face. I also observed he did not know a word of English. So, I told him in English, 'I really hope your dickhead son doesn't kill anyone else when he wraps the Audi around a telephone pole at 187 miles an hour.'

'What's that? I don't understand *gweilo*.'

I switched back to Mandarin.

'I said, I wish you and your family all the very best.'

He smiled broadly, revealing missing teeth where they had rotted away.

'Thank you! Thank you! Nice to do business.'

I was instructed to wait at a small entrance behind the prison. I was alone, staring at an iron door built into a cinder block wall. The high noon sun flattened everything under its glare. The compound was in the middle of nothing but dried-out used-up land. There was the odd struggling bush. Otherwise, it was a dead place.

All the work I had done, everything I had built, led to this moment. I was frightened the Warden would renege on the deal, as sometimes happens in these things. I imagined waiting there forever until I fell to the ground. I would die of starvation and heartache waiting for her to return to me. What if she were dead already and the joke was on both of us?

Yuánfèn.

The door swung open, and a guard shoved her out of that cinder block hole as rudely as she was shoved into that police van eighteen years ago. I walked slowly toward her, afraid to spook her. Would she recognise me? Would she even remember us?

'*Qīnài de*?'

Drab shapeless dungarees hung on her wasted body. I reached for her. Our arms slipped tenderly around one another. Her hair was hacked short. I ran my fingers through the matted clumps. What had they done to my girl? Her breath was ragged against my neck. I felt her exhaustion like a fever and perhaps she felt mine too. Her questioning fingers followed the bandage wrapped around my hand. I had not long turned 37, and she would be 50 years-old in three days.

Happy birthday, my love.

She would not tell me all the horrors she lived through. I discovered they drugged her. It took two months of ugly withdrawal symptoms to pull her out from under the addiction and restore her health.

I secreted her out of China with the best fake passport RMB could buy. She recuperated at The Spader Clinic in Melbourne. It was quite a cultural shock for her to enjoy the tender care by Australian professionals after the cruelty of Chinese prison staff. Her room always smelled of citrus disinfectant. There was a framed print of *Starry Night* on the wall to keep her company. She was always fond of the song by Don Mclean.

A therapist named Bonnie was assigned. She spoke fluent Mandarin in soft dulcet tones.

'Was Dolly ever assaulted while in prison?'

'I don't know. She won't tell me details. She clams up when I ask.'

'I bet she does this thing where she changes the subject.'

'Yes. Exactly. Dolly loves to talk about history or quote an author…'

'… because it is easier to talk about someone else's life rather than her own?'

'Yes. She does that. Why do you ask?'

'Dolly suffers from nightmares. Sometime between three and five o'clock in the morning, she kicks at the air and screams for help. Our nurses try to calm her down, but it takes a while. We're trying to avoid using sedatives, given her history with drugs as a prisoner.'

I held my head in my hands. I imagined the worst things she may have endured in any one of the gulags.

'How is her arm?'

'They didn't splint her broken arm after her arrest. It's been set incorrectly. There are certain things she can't perform normally, but Dolly is remarkably adaptable. She finds ways of doing everything she needs to do despite the limited use of her arm. On the other hand, she seems to have recovered well from the gunshot wound in her leg. She's remarkably tough. We're all incredibly impressed.'

On the day of her release from the clinic, I was nervous as hell. Would we have to fall in love all over again? After eighteen years, was it even possible?

I brought her home to our art-deco house overlooking the Yarra River. I chose a house similar to her dream home—the one overlooking the Jinjiang River in Chengdu. It was the first time she had smiled since she stepped out of prison.

In the afternoon, I took her to a Korean salon in our neighborhood where a colorist gave her hair a fresh luster. A stylist trimmed her locks into a fetching pixie cut. She gazed into the salon mirror at her carefully tousled new hairdo and found another reason to smile.

I took our story to the Australian television station, Channel Nine, as the Beijing Olympics was about to open. I knew they would appreciate the scoop as their competition was broadcasting the perverse opening ceremony I helped design.

A lady named Tara from a current affairs program interviewed me.

'The whole world is watching a torch being passed across the world. Next week, it will light a flame in Beijing. The Chinese Government's message quite clearly is they've entered the international stage as a peaceful cooperative equal with the rest of the world. Is that the case?'

'This is a pantomime. China had to save face after Tiananmen. So, The Party courted this international event to create a spectacular diversion. I know this because I was one of their window dressers.'

'You're telling me there are conflicting signals?'

'The Chinese government has two faces, and I do not care for either of them.'

'Well, Chinese artists have fled to the West and Chinese political activists and writers have disappeared. Why is it not being spoken about at an international level?'

'Their people don't feel safe, especially their most creative and talented people. If there's a chance they'll flee elsewhere. That's what they'll choose. That's what we chose.'

'Do you think it was the right decision?'

'We will see.'

'Are you frightened?'

'I *am* frightened... for her.'

I enjoyed chatting off-camera with Tara about what it is like to openly speak truth to power without fear of reprisal. It took a while to wrap my mind around such a wild concept.

I asked that the crew edit any footage of Dolly to hide her identity. Our feature story ended with a wide shot of Dolly and I, captured from behind, walking through the Melbourne Botanical Gardens holding hands.

We celebrated the Western New Year by visiting the *Karaoke Kave* in the city. The lively atmosphere reminded me of the *Shangri-La Bar*. I marveled at how the revelry is different from Chinese New Year. Western New Year spans only a single night and has less to do with family and more about singles and couples without children. We remarked on how many young people from different races were paired together. There were no barriers between people falling in love.

A woman stepped up to the microphone and began singing a song written by Dolly's namesake. She took my hand and leaned her head into my shoulder. I heard her give a little giggle during the opening words of *Jolene* by Dolly Parton.

'Dolly, I know why you find this song so funny now.'

'Is that so? How could you even know that?'

'Did you ever write about our time together? Did you happen to keep a suitcase full of diaries?'

'You've got to be kidding me!'

'I picture you sitting on your windowsill singing your heart out, strumming away on your pipa.'

I laughed until I was short of breath, while she slapped me hard across the shoulder.

'For fucks' sake!'

Her laughter joined with mine.

We found a *ChaTime* shop that made her favorite peach oolong bubble tea in a tall plastic cup. She did not mind that it was made from powder and not fresh leaves. We walked, talked, and laughed all the way home just like in the old days in Chengdu. I wished I were trapped within this memory of a memory. The delicate pain in my heart was something more powerful than remembering. This was the pain of nostalgia—far more potent than memory alone. Nostalgia takes us to a place where we ache to return, to a place where we know we are loved.

DOLLY

I watched David from behind while he unlocked the door of our home. He threw the light switch on in the entryway and tossed his key-ring into the small stone bowl by the art-nouveau umbrella stand. My eyes fixed upon him as I closed the door behind us. A sweet and salty aroma trailed behind him. He smelled of skin warmed by the sun and washed in seawater. I imagined waves crashing upon his body among the driftwood. I watched him walk along the monochrome geometric rug. He'd developed a confident pantherine grace in the way he moved. Many things must have happened to him since he was that nineteen-year-old boy still finding his feet.

Usually, I put my shoes away in their proper place in the walk-in wardrobe. I didn't feel like being neat that night. I kicked them off into the corner of our sunken lounge.

I watched him take off his shirt. The warm light from the standing lamp traced the firm smooth contours of his chest muscles. David began each morning performing a battery of stomach crunches. All his hard work paid off. I watched the ripples across his flat tummy contract when he raised each foot to take off his shoes. I traced the line of my hips with my fingertips. I'd bought a sexy red dress from *Carla Zampatti* for our date night. It was cut from a velvety fabric that felt feline. I listened to his idle chat about the warm summer nights of late while he untied his shoelaces. His voice took on a deeper, richer timbre since the days when he was a young man. I enjoyed the new piquant edge to the words that came out of that lovely mouth. What happened to my David after the day I was locked away? What had he done in the life I didn't see that gave his voice gravitas?

Barefoot and half-naked, he strolled over to the big sliding glass doors and opened them, exposing our rear balcony. The river breeze swept over the banks and into our home. The air was suddenly perfumed with eucalyptus. I moved across the room and stood behind him. The musculature of his back was a glorious Rorschach pattern of undulating peaks and valleys. He flinched in surprise when I used my finger to draw across his back in Mandarin, 属于我 (Belongs to me).

'You'll never stop surprising me.'

'I'll never stop surprising you.'

I called out instructions to our Amazon *Echo*.

'Alexa, play *Love is Found* by Sade.'

She complied, and the room filled with a song that suited my mood. A primal beat threatened to charge like a bull, restrained only by the command of the band's chanteuse. Her voice was like a bead of warm syrup running down my spine.

Our sliding glass doors became black mirrors after the sunset. I gazed at my own abstract reflection. I saw the shape of a woman I wanted to get to know all over again. I loved my spunky new pixie hair style. The red bodycon dress showcased my coke bottle silhouette. Anyone looking at this woman would be none the wiser that my arm didn't work like it should and sometimes I needed David's help getting dressed. The sliding doors were an onyx reflecting pool. I may lose myself in my own mirror image if I weren't careful. There was anger and defiance in the set of my jaw. A fire lit in my belly. I was pissed off at all the assholes who tried to rob me of myself. I wanted to feel desired and desirable. I took off my panties.

He stepped onto our balcony, and I joined him. I raised my foot and hooked it through the lattice of the railing. I brought his hand to the inside of my thigh to remind him of how smooth my skin felt. Like many Chinese women, my legs were as smooth as a dolphin and I never needed to touch a razor.

He braced one hand around the small of my back and pulled me closer to his body. His mouth sought mine and drank from my lips as though he wanted to get drunk on me. I stroked his tongue with mine as he sucked on it and then moved to my bottom lip. He let my skin slip slowly from his mouth. He licked along the pulse point of my neck, trailing a wet line to my ear where he closed his mouth around my lobe. I squeezed his ass and pushed him backward onto our outdoor sofa.

He gazed at me and used both hands to readjust the package growing in his pants. I liked it and I told him so.

'Don't stop. Keep your hands right there. Take out your cock.'

He complied. Good boy. I've always wanted to perform a lap dance. I backed up close to where he was stroking his cock. He reached out to my ass. I smacked it away.

'No touching!'

I imagined a snake. I moved my body to the smooth and sleek voice of *Sade*. My heartbeat matched the music bouncing in the space between our speakers. I imagined an anaconda winding her way in and out of his thighs, around his taut waist, and going straight to his throat. I turned on my heel, faced him, dropped to my knees, planted my hands on his thighs, and slowly ran my breasts up the length of his cock. I got the reaction I was looking for.

'Ooops. Made you pre-cum.'

I swiped it up with my finger. He opened his mouth to laugh. I put my wet finger straight into his mouth and took off his pants.

I stood up straight. Planted one foot beside him on the couch.

'Scooch down.'

He sunk deep into the furniture.

'Further. On your knees.'

I lifted my dress, laced my fingers through his hair, and pressed his mouth into my inner thigh. He always understood how to tease me before he closed in on my pussy. I discovered his mouth and tongue were performing new tricks. I wondered about the lucky women who taught him these things while I was otherwise engaged. I felt the tender skin around my clit pull away as he sucked it into his mouth. I enjoyed seeing my hand wrapped around the back of his head. I pulled on his scalp with sudden ferocity, and then tenderly smoothed over his hair to make it all better. Waves of pleasure rolled in from the deeper parts of my ocean. I tilted my head back and cried out.

'*Qīnài de*!'

We'd only begun to get to know our neighbors. They could, if they wished, witness our shenanigans from their own balcony. Would they still invite us over for dinner as they promised?

I gently pushed him away, held his hand, and led him to the railing. I leaned against it, facing the river. I lifted my ass and rolled up the hem of my dress. He dropped to his knees again and this time I was the one who was surprised. He'd never put his tongue in my ass before that night.

'How do I taste?'

'Like an expensive dessert.'

'I'm packin' all the flavors you need, handsome.'

He threw his head back and laughed out loud into the night.

I looked out past our backyard and across the riverbank. There were a number of party boats full of NYE revellers. Their jubilations were a distant hum. Could they see us silhouetted by the light of our home? Could they see a naked man, his mouth in my ass? The thought that they might catch sight of us fired up long-forgotten pleasures. Exhibitionism always lived large in my fantasies. I wanted to be heard, caught, seen, exposed and displayed. It was a compulsion to scandalize myself, an urge to outrage, a fetish of defiance.

I gave the party people a show. I pushed David back onto the couch and fucked him reverse cowgirl. In the old days when I did this, I used to plant my hands on his chest behind me. Since the massacre, one of my arms refused to cooperate with me. I adjusted by shifting my weaker arm to cradle my boobs. I thought it looked cooler that way, anyway.

It was an extra kick that I was clothed while he was naked. He reached around and found my nipples, kneading and pulling on their flesh through the delicate film of my red dress. I bucked and flexed my pussy around his cock. This elicited a loud moan from him, which only made me grin and do it again. Soon, creamy white streaks of my girl-cum were smeared up and down his cock. Wet sounds combined with my whorish moans and his wanton groans. I tried tilting my hips to create even more friction, clenching my muscles around him. I wanted every part of him rubbing against every part of me. I tore off my dress. I heard the ripping of fabric, but I was beyond caring about a thousand-dollar garment. His hard muscles ground against my soft curves. While I planted my pelvis into his lap, he reached around my body and rubbed small circles over my clit, urging me on. The doubled sensation caused a cry to build in my throat. I felt a familiar swelling from inside me. I was desperate to have him follow me, like we always did, running towards the edge together.

A tsunami wave crested over, and I rode its terrible beauty. A scream tore from my mouth, giving my ecstasy a voice. My legs shook in a violent rhythm, and with each spasm, my muscles clamped down onto his cock. I squirted all over his thighs and over our timber decking. The mess I made served to hasten his own undoing. I was aware of him following me, his arms wrapped around me as his body broke into mine. He whispered my name like a prayer as he emptied all his hot cum inside me. The neighbors will definitely not invite us for dinner now.

I lay sated in a soft boneless heap across his hard body. We were still joined, as if afraid to let go of the moment. His labored breathing syncing with mine. The sweat from our bodies cooled in the breeze from the Yarra River.

It was midnight. The New Year's fireworks lit up the sky and covered us in all the colors. That was the year David and I turned 45 and 57.

I spared a thought for my fellow parlor girls that I left behind a lifetime ago. I missed them. I wished them every happiness. I wished somewhere out there Cici was sitting in an alfresco cafe in Rome, chain-smoking while watching the nuns stroll by. Her truth hidden behind her big dark sunglasses. I wished for Lily to find her stallion. I imagined them galloping across a Spanish plain, her hair flying free.

DAVID

The next morning, the radio was playing a song released soon after Dolly was taken. I heard her crooning to Linda Ronstadt in the shower. I stood in our bathroom doorway. The shower glass fogged and dripped with steam. Behind its prism, her silhouette was a dance of curves in the shape of a woman. This was my dearest memory—the radio, the running water, and her singing. I joined in on the chorus of *All My Life.*

Wabi-Sabi contacted me and asked if I would like to reveal I was the chief architect for our graphics tablet. By then, designers all over the world considered our tablet as an essential tool. The partners felt it was only fair for me to share the credit. I agreed and the market value doubled as soon as the brand *Gossamer* appeared on the next generation of tablets. I gave a quote to *Forbes* magazine.

China's most talented ballet dancer, Li Cunxin, got the hell out of that country and is now living his best life here. The Chinese government could avoid losing so much talent if they weren't a Party of thugs.

My public fuck-you to the Communist Party felt deeply satisfying. It was the perfect denouement to the story of our escape from the regime. Was I tempting fate? What if The Party decided to make an example of me and/or Dolly? Their people are all over the globe. Others disappeared for lesser things.

After were sitting on a picnic blanket in our backyard. Our traditional Chinese tea set was laid out. Our lawn was like a thick green shag carpet. The shadows were cut sharp by the bright sun. The novelty of owning a lawn! Until we moved to Australia, we never claimed a piece of the Earth.

'David, now I know that you snooped in my diaries and violated my private thoughts, it's only fair you reveal something secret as well.'

She grinned with all the sexy mischief of the woman I first met a lifetime ago.

'Challenge accepted. I'll be right back.'

I stood, walked inside, and returned minutes later with one of my old art journals. I wiped away the dust, cracked it open, and began reading,

'*She bites her nails. It's a revealing compulsion. Why is she driven to groom past the point of usefulness?*'

'You know, the practice goes back three millennia. The ancient Greek philosopher Cleanthes, was addicted to biting his nails.'

I shook my head, laughing.

'I knew you'd say something like that. Anyway, may I finish?'

'Please continue.'

'*I treat her vulnerability with an open heart. Is there some way to tell her it's okay to be at her wit's end and not feel less than the awesome person I love? I am not frightened by the fragile person she tries to hide from me. I love the sad child I glimpse beneath the everyday resourceful grown-up.*'

By the time I finished reading, she was curled up in my lap.

We enjoyed a handful of years together. One day she told me she was not feeling well. This day turned into a week. A week stretched into a month. I became quite adept at telling if she was

hiding pain. I wondered if she was aware of how cruel it was to fill me with the false hope she was getting better? I could tell nothing was getting better.

The drugs, the abuse, the neglect, and last of all, heart disease had taken a toll. Last spring, she managed to enjoy a daily walk along the Yarra River. By winter she was too weak and exhausted from both the disease and the barrage of treatments.

She did, however, enjoy spending her days sitting on our veranda with me. She could not get enough of the crystal-clear Australian skies. The light saturated all the colors of our neighborhood. We discovered this is why the Australian suburbs are painted by artists in sharply defined hues.

I often stood behind her and massaged her shoulders.

'You know, I can no longer feel that knot in the space between your nape and left rhomboid. Were you getting massages in prison?'

She laughed at my dodgy joke.

'*Shén jīng bìng*!'

(Mental case)

I enjoyed serving her breakfast of tea and fruits in our stark white retrofitted kitchen. It was heartbreaking when she told me she could only stomach the oolong tea I would brew for her. Some days she drank only half a cup.

Her hospice nurse was a gentle giant named Jeremy who reminded Dolly of Rodin's *The Thinker*. One morning, as he was organizing her meds in our kitchen, she asked him a question.

'How will it feel when my body begins to shut down?'

She spoke with general practitioners, cardiologists, nurses, and surgeons at three different clinics. Not once had anyone spoken with her about what would happen as she died.

Jeremy took a thoughtful moment, then offered his best answer.

'Roughly in the last fortnight until the last moments, people become too sick and delirious to tell us what they're going through. We only know what dying looks like rather than what it actually feels like.'

I spent the summer finding out what it looks like.

One day she stayed in bed and so I stayed as well. She asked me to dress her in her best pajamas. They were striped in two shades of pink with a little dachshund stitched on the pocket. Her voice was weak. I had to lean in close to her so she could whisper in my ear.

'Draw me a pair of kites flying above the trees. One kite is a butterfly. The other is a bird made of all the colors you have in that box of yours. They catch and hold the wind like they're never coming down.'

She stopped breathing before I could finish the drawing.

There was not a cloud in sight at her funeral. The sky was as blue as I felt inside. I was angry the weather was pretending everything was great when she was leaving me. This time I could not rescue her.

I found myself obsessing over the weeds in our garden. There was an infestation of chickweed which needed dusting with ammonium sulfate in the spring before it germinated. I found a rash of pigweed that could be controlled with a pre-emergence herbicide containing trifluralin. Dolly and I spent many afternoons nurturing our garden. I was determined not to let it go like this.

My counselor told me I may feel a displaced need to be supportive of others and suppress my own grief. However, I had no one else to support. It was only Dolly and I living our little life together. We were two runaways who had only each other. Consequently, I had nobody else to support me, and I needed it so much. There were only those who were paid to do so. I was alone again like that boy who sketched faces in her doorway. I was terrified of her leaving me because I built my life around her. Everything I made, all of this, was only so she would be by my side.

I stopped obsessing over the chickweeds and pigweeds in our garden. It was no longer our garden. It was only my garden now.

Dolly never got to meet the friends I made after she died. There were things I should have said to her, but I let the moment escape me. There were things we should have done together, but I thought we had more time. There were things she needed from me and things I should have given, but I did not know she would leave me so soon.

DOLLY

David, you were the hero I needed you to be. What did it cost you? Your eyes no longer turned emerald green like they used to in the old days. Something was stolen from you in the interim. I'm more sad about this than the bullet hole in my leg or my arm that no longer works like it should. I want you to understand you have made my exit from this life the best years of my life. I already had the wings, but you helped me to fly.

DAVID

Hauling open the big door to my Melbourne studio was becoming more difficult of late. It was solid timber and reinforced with cast iron brackets. The building was a repurposed textile warehouse off Flinders Lane. There was a time, years ago, when I could shove it open with ease.

I entered my studio via a laneway layered in startling graffiti of every color I have ever known. Once inside, my senses were neutralized by the absence of all color. Stark white walls rose to meet a pure white high ceiling. Skylights flooded the space with sunlight or moonlight. It was far more cheerful and far less daunting than the cluttered dungeon of my old Beijing workshop. The vast floor space was sparingly furnished with an inclined draftsman's desk, a terribly accurate and expensive pigment printer, and an ergonomic swivel chair that looked as if it was designed by *NASA*. The desk cradled two giant prototype touch screens built by my brand. They made use of two-billion colors. The prototype stylus could sense ten-thousand pressure levels. It was light-years from the modest *Rand* gadget I tinkered with in that musty storeroom decades ago.

One day, I welcomed a visitor from the Royal Melbourne Institute of Technology. They were a Chinese-Australian student who was working on their Masters in Design. Academia was a lifetime ago for me. I wondered how things changed since the days when you touched a pencil and not a screen. The young student asked about the only thing I placed on my wall—a grid of one-hundred *Polaroid* photographs of the same woman.

'This was Dolly.'

'Your wife?'

'It never occurred to us to marry.'

'I don't think I'll marry my partner, but I'd like to grow old with him.'

'She always joked she wanted me to live longer than her because she didn't want to ever feel lonely again.'

I took down the *Polaroid* photograph of her sitting by the Funan River in a rickshaw wearing big ugly glasses and a tired smile. I took a breath and let it go—long and deep. Time slowed down. I wept while holding her picture in my old hands.

Begun 6th January, 2021.

Completed 23rd November, 2024.

Zee

The Cover Drawing

Charcoal no.55
Artist: Lee Woodman
Original held in private collection
Reproduced with artists permission.

I chose Lee's work because he made it with his hands and real charcoal. I imagine the fine black dust spilling off the paper and floating through the air. His work is a wonderful mess in a way that only the human eye, heart and hand may understand. I wanted something that was not plotted on an computer screen. How would I know if the "artist" hasn't let A.I do most of the work?

A.I is derivative and predictable by nature. It copies, pastes and panders because the tech bro who built the thing is trying to get rich. This is bad news only for the artist who is derivative, predictable and trying to get rich. The artist who surprises people with things nobody expected will be the artist who survives AI.